QUARK'S BAR WAS FULL OF KLINGONS.

But Worf knew exactly who he was looking for. He stepped forward and addressed the Klingon soldier. "You are Drex, son of Martok," he stated flatly.

The other Klingon surveyed him with disapproval. "That is right."

"I am Worf, son of Mogh," Worf said. Then, without further announcement, Worf slammed Drex full in the face, knocking him hard against the bar with a clatter of glassware. Stunned, Drex clawed for his dagger, but Worf struck first, his fists flying. Drex slumped to the deck, unconscious. Worf spun around instantly, knowing what was coming toward him—all the other Klingons in the bar. All unhappy with what he had just done. . . .

Look for STAR TREK Fiction from Pocket Books

Star Trek: The Original Series

Star Trek: The Next Generation

Star Trek: Deep Space Nine

Star Trek: Voyager

STAR TREK
DEEP SPACE NINE®

THE WAY OF THE WARRIOR

A Novel by Diane Carey
Based on *The Way of the Warrior* written by
Ira Steven Behr & Robert Hewitt Wolfe

POCKET BOOKS
New York   London   Toronto   Sydney   Tokyo   Singapore

An *Original* Publication of POCKET BOOKS

POCKET BOOKS, a division of Simon & Schuster Inc.
1230 Avenue of the Americas, New York, NY 10020

STAR TREK is a Registered Trademark of
Paramount Pictures.

A VIACOM COMPANY

This book is published by Pocket Books, a division of
Simon & Schuster Inc., under exclusive license from
Paramount Pictures.

ISBN: 0-671-56813-2

First Pocket Books printing October 1995

10 9 8 7 6 5 4 3 2 1

POCKET and colophon are registered trademarks of
Simon & Schuster Inc.

Printed in the U.S.A.

PART
ONE

CHAPTER
1

"WE'VE GOT TO do better than this."

Phaser rifles. Lightweight, efficient, somehow unassuring at the moment. They'd been modified, but not tested.

The test was everything. The test was the future. Captain Benjamin Sisko hungered to pull the trigger, try the weapon on the creature who threatened his station. There was just no simulation for that.

His dark skin was rosined with sweat, his attitude charred. He felt the sweat and saw it reflected in glassy access portals as he crept past. They'd been at this for hours. So far, no improvements.

He paused and crouched at a junction. The space station's dismal corridors were guerrilla paradise, and that was both helpful and prohibitive. Unfortunately, given the talents of his enemy, the old station might very well aid the evil. That was the personality of *Deep Space Nine*. It was his to possess, as long as he could hold its slippery hand.

Dodging down another length of corridor, he glanced behind him. At his flank, the slender form of Kira Nerys was barely a sliver of shadow. Grim and focused, she was slowing down after all these hours on the hunt, he could tell. And so was he.

She was good at this, though. Of course, she had done it half her life, on the planet slowly turning nearby. But that was the past, and this was the bitter present.

Ben Sisko reached a doorway and flattened against the bulkhead on the far side. Kira did the same on the opposite side. He nodded to her, held up his hand, and counted one-two-three with his fingers. His hand closed into a fist.

The major struck the comm panel with her palm.

The door washed open and all secrets were blown.

Together they swung inside, leading with their rifle barrels. Sisko opened fire.

An expanding burst of energy flowered into the quarters, swallowing every inch from floor to ceiling, draping the walls, caressing the furniture.

After the burst, Sisko stopped, and waited. Beside him, Kira was breathing hard.

Nothing happened. The enemy wasn't here. Again.

On his heaving chest his comm badge whimpered for attention. *"O'Brien to Sisko."*

"Go ahead," Sisko said, unhappy with what he was going to say.

"We've swept all of level seventeen. No sign of the changeling."

"Move down to eighteen," Sisko said. That order got him off the hook of having to say he hadn't had any success either. They *had* to do better than this. Couldn't fight what they couldn't even find. "We'll meet you there after we finish checking the guest quarters."

"Just watch yourself, Chief," Kira said. "This changeling knows the station as well as we do. He could be anywhere. Or anything."

The painfully obvious. She was either annoyed or joking—Sisko couldn't tell. Her voice was raspy, unreadable.

"Aye, Major."

Sisko motioned for Kira to follow. They would keep doing this until it worked. The only hard fact on their side was that the changeling had to be here somewhere. He could appear as almost any object of almost any size, but one thing remained faithfully constant—he *had* to be here.

Clinging to that lacy truth, Sisko led the way to the next guest quarters. One room at a time, until they ran out of phaser power. Then it would all be over.

The next door gasped open and they charged in, but this time, before Sisko could fire, a chair—and not a very attractive furnishing at that—suddenly blended out of form and into a jet of red-orange protoplasmic liquid. It arched over their heads as they ducked, then in midflight changed again, this time to the form of a bird. And out into the corridor, and away.

Gone, before they could get off a shot.

Grinding his teeth, Sisko hit his comm badge. "We found him! He's headed for the Promenade!"

Together in their anger and frustration, he and Kira

plunged down the corridor, trying to anticipate the moves of a creature so alien from themselves that it didn't even breathe. How could they think like that?

"This is giving me a stomachache," Kira growled as they ran. "There's got to be a better way to fight changelings."

"Obviously conventional weapons aren't going to be the way," Sisko heaved. "We have to be more creative than they are. And with beings who can turn themselves into any form, that's going to take some creating."

Wiping sweat from her cheek as they came out into the open area of the Promenade, Kira snarled, "I don't know if I'm all that imaginative."

She was furious and Sisko didn't blame her. That was fine—he'd rather have her on his side and mad. There was too much on the line.

They came out onto one of the overhead walkways and made their way toward the stairs that led down into the main Promenade, running past two-person security teams also armed with phaser rifles.

Below, standing in front of a shopping directory, a lieutenant was joyfully directing the action, seeming to thrive in his position at the middle of action. His wavy brown hair glinted in the unaccommodating Promenade lights, and his eyes danced.

"All right," he said, "I want phaser sweeps of everything in the Promenade. He's here somewhere . . . let's find him. On three. . . . One . . . two . . ."

His mouth made the shape of the *three,* but his voice was choked off.

Above, Sisko almost yelled out a warning, but there was no point.

An arm came around Julian Bashir's narrow shoulders and fixed beneath his chin, then pulled him sharply off balance. The shop directory itself had grown that long arm, too late for anyone to move in. They had failed miserably, and now the changeling had a hostage.

CHAPTER
2

TENSION, LOSS, DEFEAT. The terrible ring of those was a knell of the damned.

Before anyone else could move, Chief O'Brien appeared suddenly from behind a towering cactus plant and pointed his phaser rifle into the face of the changeling as the entity took human form with a punctuating slurp.

"Bang," O'Brien said. "You're dead."

"And so is Dr. Bashir," the changeling said with bitter victory. He withdrew his facsimile of an arm and set the chagrined doctor on his feet.

His gut grinding with aggravation, Sisko dropped from the stairway and hurried to them.

Behind him, Kira tapped her comm badge. "Computer, elapsed time?"

"Three hours, twenty-seven minutes."

"That's not good enough," the changeling said. "If one of my people were loose on the station for that long, there's no telling what damage he could do."

"Schedule another surprise drill," Sisko said harshly. "If the Dominion tries to infiltrate the station, I want to be ready for them."

Big words after such a big failure. He'd just lost his doctor and control of the station's central area to the enemy. He glared briefly at Security Chief Odo and couldn't help but feel a twinge of bitterness that the shapeshifter had so thoroughly faked them out. That was Odo's job, of course, and his conviction, but somehow Sisko endured a moment of irrational hostility.

"And remind everyone," Odo was saying, "that next time they'd better sweep *everything*. A changeling can be anything. A post, a pillar . . . even a patch of reflective surfacing." He tapped the directory that had served as his hiding place.

"We get the message, Constable," Chief O'Brien muttered.

"I hope so, Chief," Odo crackled with that sandpaper voice. "Just remember, the Founders are even better shapeshifters than I am."

His masklike face, smooth as putty, was enough reminder of that. They'd been fooled in the past by shapeshifters who could replicate alien features better than Odo could. What he did was natural, but untrained, like a soprano voice without a concert hall.

But today it had been enough to make fools of Sisko and his security efforts. He'd lost the station, and only the charity of simulation had left it in his hands.

He turned to leave, and flinched when someone was

standing in his way who a moment ago hadn't been there—Quark.

"Excuse me," the slippery barkeep said, "but if you're done scaring my customers away, I'd like to reopen the bar."

Kira said, "Go right ahead."

"Thank you." The Ferengi swung to Odo. "Constable, it just occurred to me that if I knew in advance how long it would take them to catch you during the next drill, well, let's just say you and I could split a substantial profit."

Irritated already by having to play the bad guy because his own people had become those, and perhaps by Quark's double-tonguing, Odo stiffened and walked away without a word.

The guileful Ferengi grinned, then added a final pinch. "Think about it!"

He varnished his win with a glance at Sisko and Kira, satisfied with himself that somehow he'd gotten a moment's enjoyment out of a morning without profit, and also left.

Sisko didn't say anything. He stepped to one side and let Kira take charge of the Security troops as they gathered around.

"Performance reviews will be held starting at oh-eight-hundred tomorrow in the wardroom," she said. "Check with your team leader for the schedule. Dismissed."

The words dropped like pebbles on the tightly woven carpet. No one was satisfied. They had just bet their lives and lost.

When Kira turned to Sisko, he could tell that she was embarrassed at their failure. She was his second-in-command. She was supposed to be able to deliver success.

He remembered that feeling from his past. It was no fun.

"How about some dinner?" she asked, avoiding talking about the drill, at least for now. Avoiding saying the things they would have to say later, that their security measures, never mind their defense grid, had just been proven full of holes. If Odo could get away from them, as he'd pointed out himself, then a fully experienced shapeshifter could turn *Deep Space Nine* into a circus.

But how could they fight aliens quite that alien? What weapons would make them cower? The phaser rifles offered a sense of security, but even shooting one of those creatures wouldn't necessarily destroy it. They worked on a whole different plane of reality, where physics was suspended and science was turned on its ear.

Fight them . . . how?

"Not tonight," Sisko said past his thoughts. "I've got a previous engagement."

"Oh, that's right," Kira said. "Captain Yates got in this morning." She smiled, relieved to have a change of subject. "Give her my regards."

Handing her his phaser rifle as if shedding himself of baggage, Sisko returned the smile, but it was a sham. "I will," he said.

But I'll keep the day's adventures to myself.

Candles in space. The technology of twenty civilizations around him, keeping him alive, giving him purpose, and still like so many others he reverted to the simple easy silence of a candle flame when inner peace was elusive. He didn't ask himself whether he would've lit the candles if Kasidy weren't coming here tonight, whether he would instead have sat in dimness, combing again and again in his mind the activities of the day, and the damnations of how to defend against the unstoppable. There had to be some way to beat the Founders without wasting effort just finding them. Some way to reach them on their own level—

Nope, the salad fork went on *that* side.

The door chimed, and suddenly his only thought was getting the table setting right. His mind was snapping, that was it.

"Come in," he said, then had a flash of panic—had he remembered to change into his civvies? Yes.

"Hello, Ben," the woman in the doorway shadow said. "I hope I'm not too late."

She was gorgeous. Exotic. Winsome. Or maybe he was just hungry for a reason to be happy.

Yet even as he strode toward her, he was wishing the dam would burst and whatever was boiling in the quadrant would simply happen and be dealt with, live or die. The waiting was ghastly.

But she was here now. . . .

"Some things are worth waiting for," he uttered to her, and surprised himself with a genuine smile this time. He scooped up a small present on the table. "Here," he said. "For you."

She smiled too, and the candles fell to shame. "Isn't that a coincidence? I have something for you, too."

With the unceremonious efficiency of captains, they handed each other their gifts and opened them.

As she drew a band of fabric from the wrapping,

Kasidy reacted to the scarf as if it were much more than a scarf. "Where'd you find Tholian silk?"

"The Tholian ambassador owed me a favor."

She accepted his explanation and slipped the scarf around her neck. The color erupted to life against her complexion. He was glad he hadn't picked the purple one.

"May I?" he asked, and held up his gift.

"It's not silk," she said, "but I think you'll like it. It's from my brother's team."

"Pike City Pioneers!" Sisko beamed as he pulled out the baseball cap with the team logo on the front.

"My brother says if you're ever on Cestus Three, he'll get you seats in the dugout."

The hat was a perfect fit, despite Sisko's newly shaven head, it'd be perfect. "How far is it to Cestus Three?"

"Eight weeks at maximum warp."

As he pulled off the hat and studied it wistfully, Sisko shook his head. "To see a real baseball game . . . might be worth the trip."

"Tell you what," she offered warmly, "if you ever decide to go, I'll take you there myself. As long as you don't mind traveling by freighter."

"I might just take you up on that." He didn't dare admit to her that it sounded like paradise at the moment, to abandon his concerns and responsibilities and drift off on some ship into the eternal darkness, at the end of which was a good old-fashioned ball game.

"Did you do this all yourself?" Kasidy was picking at the table spread.

"My father always says the way to a woman's heart," Sisko crooned, "is through her stomach."

Well, that was almost trite enough.

She didn't seem to notice. "Ah," she said, "so it's my heart you're after. . . ."

They fell into each other's eyes and briefly were caught there, lost in the fine fibers of a web they both knew was there in the evening dimness.

She broke away first, only a second or two—Sisko found himself lingering.

"In that case," she was saying, "maybe you could tell me what all those maintenance crews are doing in the docking ring."

"Just some retrofitting," he offered, and occupied himself in opening and pouring the wine.

She didn't settle for that.

"Now you *are* keeping a secret," she said. She closed in on him, delivering the silent persistence of the kind of woman he liked.

"Let's just say," he began again, "we're preparing a few surprises in case the Dominion comes through the wormhole."

Kasidy brought down one of her straight eyebrows and crimped her mouth. "Seems like everyone's got the Dominion on their minds these days. I hear the Cardassians have even sealed their borders."

Sisko offered a sympathetic shrug toward those to whom a year ago, maybe a month ago, he would rarely have found sympathy. "They're worried about being infiltrated by the Dominion. The idea that there might be changelings loose in the Alpha Quadrant has everyone a little nervous."

This wasn't what he wanted to be talking about—

the business of the quadrant dropped at his door every moment of every day, because he was the gatekeeper at one of its most dangerous gates. Once in a while a man deserved to forget that, even for a few minutes. Vigilance was his lot and ordinarily he didn't mind. But today he was mad at it.

"All I know is," Kasidy said, "I've got a cargo hold full of Teresian hardwood bound for Cardassia Prime, and now I can't deliver it. If you ask me, I think everyone's being a little paranoid." She paused. "Aren't they?"

Uneasy to be the quadrant's barometer, he resisted her searching gaze. He wanted to tell her the attitudes she was reading were nothing more than fears mustered by rumormongers, people whose daily routine was dull and who clung to every thread of interest that came their way. "I hope so," he said, knowing he wasn't fooling her. "What do you say we forget about business?"

He raised his glass. They each took a sip of wine.

Kasidy drew a long breath and relaxed. "I'd say that's a good idea."

It was a wonderful idea for the four seconds it lasted.

The comm line twittered just when things were getting nice.

"Dax to Sisko."

Sisko who? Nobody here by that name.

But it was Dax, not anyone else who might be inclined to disturb them unnecessarily. Dax was the heartbeat of *Deep Space Nine,* and she wouldn't call unless the whole station were on fire.

These days . . . it could happen.

He leaned forward. "Go ahead."

"I think you'd better get up here."

"Oh my way." He sprang to his feet. "I'll be back as soon as I can."

"I know you will," Kasidy called as he dodged out the door, and something about her voice said she really did understand, that she had been forced to rush in the same way to her own bridge in moments of crisis.

Yes, she understood. So why did he feel so empty as he plunged toward the turbolift, imagining her sitting alone at the beautiful dinner table with the beautiful stew he'd made himself?

Hungry was a rotten way to rush to Ops.

As such, the operational center of *Deep Space Nine* was wholly unwelcome as his lift doors parted and dumped him there.

Lieutenant Commander Jadzia Dax was at the Ops table, bringing a Grecian elegance to the hard alien place with her ever-classic manner. She didn't seem surprised to see Sisko here so fast, and she didn't apologize for disturbing his first dalliance in many weeks. She didn't say a thing, in fact.

She looked at him, then with her own eyes guided his gaze to the main viewscreen.

Hovering off his station as if suspended in time, masked in its own silence, was a Klingon attack cruiser.

"It just decloaked," Dax said simply. A plain statement with an uncomplicated message, except that Sisko knew Dax well and she was giving him a set of unpleasant facts that could fester if he didn't handle them correctly.

The Klingon cruiser had just come out of cloak here, very close to the station, without announcing its approach. And why would it be cloaked in allied space?

Evidently, it wasn't here to deal with allies.

"That's the new Klingon flagship," Sisko said.

"The *Negh'Var*," Dax said. "There's a General Martok aboard, asking to speak to you."

A little late.

Sisko felt his jaw take a set. "Put him through."

CHAPTER
3

GENERAL MARTOK GAZED with the satisfaction of good drink at the lonely spiral that these days was called *Deep Space Nine*. There were no markings that showed the station to be a Federation outpost. It might as well still be Cardassian, for all its outward witch-gray hull and loamy shadows.

Such a creature, that station. There were few of them, and this the first he had seen himself. Any others were still within Cardassian space.

An appealing design, this clawed monster. Three curved docking pylons launching downward from its central spool like an insect's legs in repose, and three upward—like an insect in death.

Martok smiled. Ironic.

In his mind he enjoyed what the Starfleet controllers of that station were seeing right now, and saw in his mind their faces. They might be allies for this moment, but the Klingons still had their fangs. Not long ago, such a scene would have meant the deaths of all Starfleeters who saw it.

"Get me Commander Kaybok," he said to the bridge officer in front of him.

His private screen flickered, and his fleet commander's face appeared. *"Kaybok."*

"Kaybok, let these be your standing orders. No ships may leave this area, but especially the ship that just pulled in."

"The freighter, General?"

"Yes, the freighter *Xhosa*. It's been in Cardassian space and is headed there again. When it leaves, I want you to follow it out into the sector, then stop it and search it. If there will be a leak, it will be there."

"General," Kaybok said, his brow tight, *"I do not know what I am searching for."*

"For changelings, Kaybok."

"But . . . a changeling can be . . . anything. A floor, a boot, a cup . . ."

"Yes. For the first time, we cannot be sure who our enemies are. You never know where you'll find a changeling. This is unlike any enemy we have ever fought."

"What shall I do, then?"

Martok paused. There was no good answer for this. What to do against an enemy who could sneak away as the very clothes he himself might be wearing?

"Follow your orders," he said. "Even the station may be controlled by changelings by now. Keep alert. We must find out who is the enemy."

Kaybok appeared dismayed, but nodded sharply. *"Yes, General."*

"Martok out."

"General." His ship's space master turned and interrupted. "The station is accepting our hail. Shall I instruct the rest of the fleet to come out of cloak?"

"No, Drex. Leave the cloaks on, except for vessels I will give specific instructions about. The longer we keep these people in darkness, the more our advantage will be. I want them to know what they have at their door, but not be able to count."

"I understand, General."

"Well that you do."

"Sir," Drex began, moving to him and lowering his voice, "why are we threatening a Federation station? I am your second-in-command. You should tell me."

"Only the commanders know everything, Drex," Martok said roughly. "For you, I have an assignment. I want to know what kind of weapons are on this station. You find out."

Drex's mouth fell open, but only for a second. "How shall I find out?"

"I will give you names. The pressure you put on them is your choice. You must work quietly."

With a temperate nod, Drex briefly flared at the idea of putting pressure on somebody; then he drew back as if realizing what had just been ordered.

"Are we now spying on our allies, General?"

Martok leaned toward him. "Very carefully. After all, how many die not from frontal assault, but by a stab in the back while fighting? I want to find out how long Sisko's blade is. Now, keep your voices down . . . and let me speak to him."

"Captain Sisko, I bring greetings from your allies in the Klingon Empire."

"Welcome to *Deep Space Nine*, General," Sisko offered by rote, measuring his words. He would respond politely to the so-called greeting, but without naïveté. If Martok's blunt entry into the sector was meant to convey some covert message, then there would be the same kind of message awaiting him here. "Is there something I can do for you?"

"It has been a long journey," Martok said. *"My men require shore leave."*

Sisko felt Dax shift slightly at his side, the tiniest hint that she also had suspicions. The most obvious—the Klingon mentioned how long his journey had been, but made no explanation of why he had made so long a journey. Sightseeing?

"Certainly," he said with control. "They can come aboard whenever they like."

"Good," Martok responded. He barked a command in Klingon to someone Sisko couldn't see on the screen.

Sisko knew the word—*uncloak.*

Didn't make sense. The ship already was out of cloak.

The answer wasn't pleasant, Sisko found, as a moment later he and Dax stood staring at the main screen, which showed quite passively the full scope of not one ship, not two or three, but a full Klingon task force rippling out of cloak.

* * *

"Too much for you, Captain Sisko?"

Martok's voice overlaid the scene before them, his words spoken with the smallest hint of espionage. He enjoyed what he had put before them.

The scene was imposing and unprecedented. For years—how many?—no Klingon fleet of that size had been assembled, at least none that Starfleet had any knowledge about, and Starfleet was not ignorant.

And now here they were, ship after ship, crowded on the approach lanes to *Deep Space Nine*.

Intercepting Dax's glance, Sisko felt his suspicions confirmed. Before them was certainly no fishing trip the Klingons were enjoying. No packet run, no supply line.

"This is a Federation station," Sisko said with a touch of flippancy, "manned by a full complement of Starfleet personnel. We pride ourselves on being able to handle almost anything, General. Feel free to bring your men here for shore leave. They will be met at the docking ring by our Security teams, with whom they can check their energy weapons."

For a moment there was silence over the scene before them, hovering firepower enough to rip apart entire solar systems.

"I understand," Martok's voice came back.

"I look forward to meeting you. Screen off," Sisko grumbled. He turned around, leaned back on the Ops table, and let his expression turn hard.

"That was subtle," Dax said, her lovely mouth turned up in—well, it wasn't exactly a smile.

Sisko folded his arms. "How many of them are there?"

She touched the panel before her and waited for the

readout. "I can't get a clear reading. Sensors are reading at least fourteen vessels in the immediate vicinity. That's not counting any that may still be cloaked." She looked up. "You're going to let them flood the station with their crews?"

"I haven't got a reason not to. It's one of those little thorns in the bush called alliance. It looks pretty until you stick your hand in."

Dax flickered an eyebrow. "Why so many ships?"

He shook his head. "Nobody needs that many ships. Put the station on silent yellow alert. Notify no one but security personnel and arm them with hand phasers. I don't want the Klingons to realize we're on alert status. They'll take that as an affront."

"But you don't trust them?"

"Hell, no, I don't trust them. I'll trust them the minute they explain why they're roaming my sector with a full task force."

"You won't trust them then," Dax said.

He looked at her, and for an instant, the shortest of moments, he saw not the lithe dark-haired woman who was too young for her job, but the clever and ancient trickster he had known for more years than Jadzia had been alive. Curzon Dax had found his own way to be ageless, and probably would have even if he hadn't been a Trill. These aliens and their conscience-transferring ways, the creature living inside Jadzia, possessing the thoughts of other lifetimes . . . for an instant all this seemed at Sisko's fingertips, as if he too could be one of them.

Sometimes he felt that close to Curzon. The old man's personality embraced Jadzia like scandal.

Then her gossamer cheek picked up a flash of

technical lighting from the opposite side of Ops, and reality crashed in. Any sane man would have wanted her to be exactly what she was, and here he was wishing she were a withered codger for whose memories she was the current receptacle.

She was watching him. Yeah, that was Curzon's look. "How was your date with Captain Yates?"

"Short, that's how. Damned short." He let out in his tone, and knew Dax would pick up, the level of his suspicions. "Let's hope it's not short and damned. Get the station ready. And I want to talk to Odo."

Quark's bar wasn't the best saloon in memory, but in the desert of space any watering hole could become an oasis, given enough time. Chief Miles O'Brien figured he'd anointed this dump enough that it ought to be given a proper Dublin pub name, and maybe a painted heraldic insignia.

Now, how would that look? A charming old-time heraldic shield, decorated with a couple of Ferengi ears and a pocket with a hand stuck in it.

I need a hobby.

Enough concentration. He struck the back of his own wrist. A Gramillion sand pea flipped from the back of his hand into the air. He kept his eye on it as it soared, then snapped like a bass.

"Chief," Julian Bashir said from the other side of the small table, watching O'Brien as he laboriously chewed the pea he could've swallowed whole, "I'm beginning to think there's no limit to the wonders you can perform."

O'Brien sighed and wished he were somewhere else.

"That's what I like about you, Julian," he droned. "You're easily impressed."

Strange. He hadn't spoken in a normal voice. He'd nearly whispered, even leaned toward Julian just a bit, as if afraid he'd be overheard.

He glanced to one side. Julian glanced to the other. The pervasive atmosphere of being watched was enough to peel skin.

All around them were tables full of Klingons, stone-faced and huddled, their collective voices creating a surreal rumble in the bar.

And this pretending to not notice the Klingons' deliberate "act natural" poker faces was bloody not easy.

Quark showed up like a crab escaping from shore birds and put two drinks on the table between O'Brien and Dr. Bashir, and almost put one right in the bowl of peas.

"Thank you, Quark," Bashir said. "Can we get a little yamok sauce for these sand peas?"

The fishy barkeep glanced this way and that, peering at the gathering of Klingons, unhappier than he had ever been to have a full crowd.

"Quark?" Bashir persisted.

O'Brien shifted in surprise when Quark actually sat down with them. *Sat down.*

"Listen," the Ferengi said. "Do you hear that?"

Bashir looked at O'Brien.

O'Brien shrugged. He wasn't about to encourage whatever Quark was going after.

"I don't hear anything," Bashir innocently said.

"Exactly," Quark cracked. He leaned closer and his

voice fell to a hiss. "The ambient noise level in this room is less than thirty decibels! On an average day it's sixty-five. When there are Klingons in the room, it can go as high as eighty-five."

Knowing he would regret this, O'Brien concluded, "So what you're saying is . . . it's quiet in here?"

Quark's ratlike face swiveled to him, eyes like painted buttons. "Too quiet! Something is terribly wrong."

"Like what?" Bashir asked.

O'Brien winced. *Shut up, Quark, shut up.*

And why did Bashir keep prodding? Hadn't he picked up on O'Brien's lagging about here for so long? They had to let the Klingons pretend to be relaxing on shore leave long enough to give Sisko a chance to find out what was really going on, and between Quark and Bashir, the cover was going to be blown off any minute now.

"I don't know," Quark said. "But have you ever met a quiet Klingon before? And look at the way they're watching the room. It's like they're picking out targets."

Well, this had to stop.

Pretending to give way to the bloodcurdling boredom, O'Brien put on his best Quiet Man mood and rose to his feet.

Quark gasped, "What are you doing?"

"I thought I'd ask the Klingons what they're up to."

"Don't do that!"

"Why not?"

His mouth hanging open for an instant, Quark coughed up, "I don't want them to know we're on to them!"

Dropping back into his chair, O'Brien grunted, "Suit yourself."

Relieved, he sagged back in the chair and let his legs spread out under the table. He'd taken a chance, but not much of one. Quark hadn't been likely to want a brawl in his bar, never mind the decibels. Maybe now the Ferengi would shut up and quit listening too hard, and maybe the Klingons would think their act was fooling somebody.

Shifting his chair so that he could see the most Klingons with the least glancing, O'Brien went back to pretending to be minding his own business. Quite a trick, when the principal view was Bashir trying to duplicate the pea flip. Missed.

The engineer sighed. "The secret is positioning the pea correctly on your hand."

"I thought I did," the doctor said in that boyish way of his. He reached for another pea.

Quark moved the bowl away from him. "What are you two doing? I'm telling you, the Klingons are up to something!"

"Calm down, Quark," Bashir said. "The Klingons are our allies."

"They might be *your* allies, but they're not *mine.*"

"Relax," O'Brien said as if talking to himself. "If something's up with the Klingons, Captain Sisko will find out about it."

"Yeah," Quark said gutturally, "but will he tell *me?*"

The wardroom door opened with stylish silence, but in his mind Sisko imagined the faint *swish,* and before him the Klingon walked in.

General Martok came alone. No bodyguards, no escorts. Was he so lacking in trust, even of his own men?

As he came into the room, the massive, armored Klingon looked slowly to his left, to his right, and even glanced at the ceiling. His every movement was one of reined suspense. This wasn't a man on shore leave.

Aware that he might have been falling prey to his own paranoias, those that naturally came to the commander of an outpost so far out in space, a place that would've been forsaken but for the quirk of nature it guarded, Sisko thought twice about what he was seeing. Could it be that Martok was ordinarily the suspicious type? Some Klingons were. And might it be that the Klingon task force of so many ships was out for a drive?

Of course. That was it.

As such, Sisko decided that this was not some flaw in himself making him measure what he saw with so tainted an eye. He wasn't imagining a damned thing.

Nor did he miss Martok's subtle bumping of the chairs as he made his way toward Sisko and Major Kira. Finally, after looking at the walls, the chairs, the table, putting a hard heel to the carpet, he looked up at the two of them.

Sisko stepped to him. But not too close. "So, what brings you here, General?"

"A valid question," Martok said. "But first . . ." He drew his dagger, a heavy business blade that could have only one purpose, and salad wasn't involved.

At Sisko's side, Kira shifted when Martok raised the weapon and sliced a cut into his own hand. He extended the hand and let the blood drip onto the tabletop.

"Let us be sure we are who we say we are."

He handed the dagger to Sisko with a clear message of what he expected.

Kira impugned, "You think we're changelings?"

"What I think doesn't matter," Martok said. "The blood will tell."

A piece of the puzzle clicked into place. One, at least, of Martok's fears, and possibly one of his motivations, had just explained itself. Were these fears personal, or was he a carrier for wider-based concerns?

Sisko waved Kira back. With the heavy Klingon blade he cut his own hand and let the carnelian drops fall beside thistle-colored beads of Martok's blood on the tabletop.

He passed the knife to Kira, plagued only by a lingering twinge of gentlemanliness that didn't like the idea of her having to do this. She was a soldier, though, for many years longer than he had been, for she had started young. While he was enjoying the comforts of Federation-stable peace, Kira had grown up below on the planet of Bajor, fighting a day-by-day trench war for her freedom against the Cardassian occupation. She could handle one more cut.

She took a hack out of her palm, and her anger came through. With simmering wrath she smeared her blood on the table beside theirs, then looked up with an are-you-satisfied glare.

Martok bent over the blood and examined it, waiting for it to change shape, revert to metallic orange as the disembodied part of a changeling would. It didn't. It remained blood, spread slowly across the glassy tabletop, and mingled.

Relief clearly washed over him that otherwise a Klingon would tend to hide. He sat down and visibly let the tension go.

"Now that that's over," Sisko prodded as he sat, and motioned for Kira to sit also. He wanted Martok to finish the sentence.

Martok slumped back in his chair like a perverted Santa Claus waiting to hold children on his lap and bite their heads off.

"We've been sent here," he began, "to fight alongside our Federation allies against the Dominion."

Dominion . . . the Founders. Odo's people, a civilization existing with such bizarre bodily forms that physics no longer applied to them. They were the new enemies of the Federation, of the Klingons, of anyone living on this side of the natural tunnel called the wormhole. In a matter of moments anyone could go from here to a quadrant of the galaxy tens of thousands of light-years away—otherwise inaccessible. Meaning, of course, that the Dominion could come through also.

And they wanted to. With their attack dogs, the Jem'Hadar, leading the way, most likely. The only question had become the cruelest. When?

Suddenly, as he sat here staring at one of the rarest sights he'd ever seen—a frightened Klingon—Sisko was struck with the inevitability of war. When were the Founders coming? They already had spies here. It was sorcery to get used to the idea of not trusting chairs and carpets.

The Klingons, if Martok spoke for all of them and

hadn't today become a renegade, wanted to stand fast against the Dominion any way they could, even if it meant coming in here to broaden the width of the castle gate.

"I appreciate the gesture," Sisko told the general. "But I'm not sure it's necessary."

Martok was ready for that. "The Klingon High Council thinks it is."

"Our communications relay in the Gamma Quadrant hasn't detected any signs of Jem'Hadar activity for quite some time. They seem to be giving the wormhole a wide berth."

"They will come," Martok said. "And when they do, we will be ready for them."

CHAPTER
4

"GENTLEMEN, WELCOME TO my haberdashery. May I
interest you in some of Earth's Roman leg greaves? I
appropriated them from a rather excitable antiques
dealer who passed through last month. And may I say,
there's nothing more elegant for an upwardly mobile
warrior than attire from one of the most successful
imperial forces of all time—"

"We have no interest in your wares, tailor."

The Klingon spat the word *tailor* as if it were an
insult.

What a shame. No appreciation for artisanship.

Deep Space Nine's local Cardassian peered up at the
two rather wide-framed Klingons and smiled his most
saccharined smile.

"Very well . . . then what can I do for you?"

"Your name is Garak?"

He bowed in a small way. "So you can read the sign. Imagine that. Such intellect."

"You share this station with Starfleeters," the ugly one said, "yet you are an enemy alien."

"Ah, ah." Garak raised a scolding finger. "Cardassia is not, properly speaking, at war with the United Federation of Planets. Not yet, anyway. Would you gentlemen like to have your armor taken in? Perhaps a little under the arms and around the thighs. You both look a little gaunt. May I have your names, please, for the invoice?"

"I am Drex, second officer of—"

"Fool!" the other one snapped in Klingon. *"You tell him your name?"*

Garak settled one hand on his hip and waited. The Klingon language was particularly unmusical and it had been a long time since he'd used it, but this could be instructive.

These two would last about four minutes in the intelligence service, so quick were they to believe that only Klingons had the muscles or the armor or honorability or whatever it took to speak Klingon.

"He is a nothing," Drex told his friend. His mate. His excuse for a compatriot. Whatever they were to each other. Was there a word for that?

"In any case," Garak interrupted, "I can certainly sell you some new clothing. I should think you'd be embarrassed walking around like that. The 'indomitable warrior' look is out this season."

"Make him an offer!" the one with the long mustache said. *"Tell him he can have anything you want to tell him. But get it over with! I would rather just kill him and take what we need from his computer."*

"Shut up, Ruktah. Any changes in this station's armaments in the past months will be new in that computer. We need his access codes. If we kill him, we'll be put off the station."

"All right, all right. But if he smiles at me one more time I'll strangle him and his mother!"

Garak watched as they snarled at each other. Without even expecting to, he had learned what they wanted. The station's condition. Weapons. Klingons were *so* easy.

"Well?" he prickled. "Have you decided? Let me guess—you need medieval jousting helmets to cover those faces. I don't blame you. Use clothing to mask your worst features, I always say. I happen to have those right over—"

Drex charged the three steps between them and pasted Garak up against the shop's computer console. "Name your price, tailor! Share with us what you share with your keepers on this station! Give us the way into the main memory bank!"

"Oh, I would," Garak choked, "but there's a problem."

"What problem?"

"Well, you see, I just don't like you."

"You don't like Klingons?"

"Oh, no, I can live with Klingons. They huff and puff and rush in where they're not wanted, but I don't mind them. I just don't like *you.*"

Drex inhaled and drew back a hand to throttle him with, but Ruktah grabbed him by the wrist guard.

"Not now!" the other one growled in Klingon. *"We can get it somewhere else. Martok gave us more sources than this boiled Cardassian noodle."*

Lips quivering with fury, Drex managed to control himself. And what a sight it was to see.

Slowly, as his big hands trembled with rage, he let go of Garak.

"Thank you so much," Garak said through a crushed throat. "I appreciate your pressing my collar. Now I don't have to do that. This Tholian silk, you know—"

"Animal," Ruktah croaked at Garak as he dragged Drex toward the exit.

Drex shook his companion's hand off and glared at Garak. *"Useless animal."*

"Do come again," Garak called. "Tell all your charming friends. I'm open until oh-six-hundred!"

Weapons updates. Station details about changes in armaments. Whatever they wanted and whyever they wanted it, this couldn't be in his best interest, Garak pondered as the smell of them began to dissipate.

"Well, they're obviously not just on shore leave," he sighed, and tried to breathe evenly so his heart would slow its thunderous pounding.

"Memory banks . . . memory banks . . . should be simple enough," he uttered as he sat at his computer console.

He began to tap in a series of codes, data, and bank file accesses, as well as he could remember them. He would be able to get everything he needed, or at least enough to satisfy the Klingons, within an hour or so.

Then all he had to do was get those two prehistoric vandals to come back here, instead of rifling some other poor slob who would have to tell them everything in order to stay alive.

* * *

Trill public baths had quite a reputation that went beyond sensuality and uninhibitedness and into just plain comfort. In a galaxy that could offer almost anything, comfort became a simple pleasure.

People talked, laughed, splashed, swam, and their sounds echoed placidly through the large open space.

In one of the dozen steam rooms flanking the main bathing area, behind delectable hanging tapestries, Kira sat on a bench and tried to enjoy the moist heat, but the comfort wasn't sinking in. She didn't want to be here.

"There you are," a voice cut into her thoughts.

Dax came toward her, wearing a flimsy garment called a *kfta* or *takfa* or *kifata* or something. Kira found herself fixated on the word and had a fleeting thought of going to the tailor's shop and asking Garak what the thing was called. On either arm, Dax had a male Trill, and she looked particularly elegant striding among her own people. They all had that same look of diffidence.

"We've been looking all over for you," she said. "Malko here just gave me an amazing massage. I'm sure if you ask nicely he'd be willing to do the same for you."

Malko smiled to prove he would.

Kira didn't hide her sneer. "No, thanks."

"Why?" Dax persisted.

Kira lowered her chin. "Because Malko isn't real. He's a puppet made of holographic light and replicated matter."

Dax sighed, frustrated. To Malko and his counterpart she said, "Boys, can you wait outside?"

The two shrugged, not programmed to make any visitor feel bad, and strolled away.

Kira kept her gaze fixed on Dax. "Afraid I hurt their 'feelings'?"

"You really should try to get into the spirit of things," Dax said milkily as she sat down. "People come from all over Trill to visit the Hoobishan baths."

"And if I'm ever on Trill, I'll visit them too. But we're not on Trill, and this isn't the Hoobishan baths. It's a holosuite. Nothing here is real."

"And?"

Melancholy and preoccupied, Kira sighed. "I'm sorry, Dax. I just feel . . . silly."

"Good. That's what a holosuite's for. To have a good time. All you have to do is relax and use your imagination."

"I guess I don't have much of an imagination." Kira didn't mention that no amount of bathing or steaming or Malko could make her forget they were on a station in space that was overloaded with Klingons.

"Of course you do," Dax told her patiently. She knew. "Everyone does. Didn't you used to play make-believe when you were a kid?"

"Yes. I used to make believe that all the Cardassians would stop killing Bajorans and just go away."

Dax gazed at her. The smile left her face and eyes. "I'm sorry. I didn't mean—"

"No, I'm the one who's sorry. I guess I've never gotten much use out of my imagination. I mean, look at me! You planned a fun evening for us and all I can do is sit here and worry about Klingons."

"You can worry about them tomorrow," Dax said. "From what I hear, they aren't going anywhere. As for your underdeveloped imagination, I prescribe a strict regime of exercise . . . starting immediately."

Kira kept looking up at her as if she could catch the enthusiasm like a virus. But it guttered. The smile she forced up was fake. Lying around was still just lying around, and a person could only take so much of it when things were going on elsewhere, even if it was pleasant lying around.

"All right," she forced out. "I'll give it a try."

"That's all I ask." Dax stood up. "Come on. Malko couldn't have gotten far."

Kira got to her feet also. *If he did,* she thought, *then he'd better know Klingon pressure points.*

The Promenade was markedly quiet. Activity here, activity there, a few shoppers braving the imposing Klingons who meandered about with fake casualness in groups of two or three. The fact that they moved in twos and threes was itself unsettling. Such grouping was obviously forced, planned to appear haphazard.

And they rarely stopped. They walked, paused, then wandered on, like sentries on watch.

For what were they watching?

Sipping a cup of coffee, Odo was aware of every Klingon presence within eyeshot from where he sat at the Replimat. It was a good place to keep surveillance over what was happening.

Across from him, Garak was enjoying a full meal.

"Fascinating," Garak said between bites. "So both the cup and the liquid are merely extensions of your own body?"

"That's correct. And if I want to, I can even drink the liquid, reabsorb it, and produce new 'coffee' in the cup." Odo wanted to stay here without attracting attention, so entertaining Garak was as good a way as any. He took a pretend swallow of the coffee, then held out the cup to Garak, showing him that the coffee was refilled. "This way I can give the illusion that I'm sharing the dining experience."

"Very thoughtful." Garak did a poor job of showing his interest. He was no more interested than he was a tailor.

"So," Odo went on, "perhaps you'd like to tell me what's bothering you?"

Garak paused with a fork halfway to his lips. "Why do you think there's something wrong?"

"Because you're almost done with your meal. It usually takes you twice as long to eat your breakfast."

Within the Cardassian goggles of bone around his eyes, Garak blinked. "Does it?"

"In my experience," Odo went on, "most mornings you're more interested in talking than eating."

"Maybe I'm just hungry today."

Lies.

Odo couldn't blame Garak for being on edge, considering the presences added to the station's complement, but Garak was not a simple individual with simple purpose and he wasn't easily intimidated.

Gradually Odo's thoughts turned back to his own problems. Why was he plied with guilt today? He had won the game, but the drill had been a failure. He had too easily evaded the troops and captured a hostage. And even a changeling couldn't look at an object and tell if it was another changeling hiding there.

At least *he* couldn't.

He knew these people, these Federation citizens, took him as coldhearted and withdrawn, and perhaps that's what drove him to sit among them despite the urge to cloister himself. Or more—he responded to their acceptance of him. Deep-running feelings stirred in him.

Or was it guilt? He fought bitterly against feeling responsible for what the Dominion was trying to do, for the actions of other changelings, but it was hard. They were committing immoral acts. Their attempts at conquest were heinous, and he told himself over and over again that those attempts had nothing to do with him. He had learned from the Federation that there was no "group" responsibility any more than there were "group" rights. The idea that someone who looked like him could commit a crime and he would be somehow responsible—absurd! He fought to remain above that.

It was part of what he liked about the Federation. They didn't buy into that. If all the changelings were murderous thugs—and well they might be—the Federation would never take it out on him. Some individuals might, but the law never would.

But since he couldn't shake the guilt, could it be that he was failing to live up to Federation standards? Was his identification with race too strong?

Perhaps his guilt was of another color—should he have made the sacrifice of personal identity and stayed with the Founders, as they asked him to? If they were a collective consciousness as well as a collective physical form, perhaps he could have infused his ideals among them and made a difference. Or would he have been a drop in the ocean, lost completely?

He knew the Federation would never order him to lose himself in the mass, but perhaps he could still do it. Maybe it wasn't too late.

A chance to divert an entire civilization from goals of conquest . . . after all, he *had* been sent out to learn and bring back his perceptions. Instead of handing over what he had learned, he had stayed here, among unlike beings with principles the same as his own.

He didn't want to go. If he was wrong and merely became a drop in the ocean, then *Deep Space Nine* would have lost its only changeling. Life for him had been markedly better since Starfleet had taken over the station, and he felt a devotion to these people. They needed him to help man the fort and provide a glimpse into the talents of the enemy.

It wasn't much of a reason to stay, but he clung to it. He wanted to stay. Principles were everything.

Across the table, Garak indulged in a heavy breath, then asked, "Tell me, Odo, have you heard any news from Cardassia lately?"

Glad to be released from his thoughts, Odo said, "Not since they sealed their borders."

"Well, I have. And, frankly, I don't like what I've been hearing. Rumors of uprisings, civil disturbances—all very alarming."

"I didn't know you still have friends inside the Empire."

Garak rolled those animated eyes. "One or two. But now I can't even get through to them. I'm worried . . .

with the destruction of the Obsidian Order and the threat of the Dominion, these are unsettling times for Cardassia."

Gazing at him to find the layers beneath the presented surface, Odo sensed a touch of fear in Garak. Yes, Garak was hard to scare when action occurred, but this unknown, undefined threat was more frightening certainly than hard ordnance and clear enemies. Garak didn't know any more than Odo did what would come next. With the Cardassian Gestapo out of power, someone else soon would be in power.

Still staring at the Klingons out on the Promenade, Odo said, "They're unsettling times for everyone. But if I hear anything, I'll let you know. Excuse me a moment."

Something reliably concrete had just popped up.

In the Promenade, two Klingons had stopped a citizen of the station, a fellow named Morn, and they were harassing him, rifling his duffel bag, pressing him for space as if they had some right to do so.

Garak was following, but Odo didn't care. He plunged toward the Klingons, then drew up short and kept his arms at his sides.

"May I help you?" he asked, not in a very accommodating tone.

One of the Klingons, a warrior with a bitter face, glowered at him and spat a hate-dripping phrase in Klingon.

Or was it only that every phrase in Klingon sounded like an insult?

The other Klingon laughed, and both turned away.

"Actually," Garak interrupted, "I'm not sure the constable *has* a mother."

The Klingons swung back, basted with shock at a Cardassian who knew their language. They seemed to take Garak very personally for some reason.

Odo stepped between them and Garak before anything got started. "Gentlemen, if you have business on the Promenade, I suggest you go about it. If not, move along."

"I'd listen to him if I were you," Garak added in a particularly taunting manner.

The first Klingon snarled, "I don't take orders from shapeshifters . . . or their Cardassian lapdogs!"

"I may be a shapeshifter," Odo said evenly, "but I'm also chief of security of this station. So either you move along, or you'll be continuing this conversation from inside a holding cell."

With his attitude he hoped he conveyed the simple message that he would clear a cargo hold and incarcerate every Klingon in the task force to maintain peace on the station.

The Klingons held back. Odo found that unlikely and took it as a clue. These types would have been happy to start a fight just for the distraction.

They didn't. Why not? Orders?

Why would they be given such orders? Klingon commanders generally didn't care about fallout from the actions of their men.

"As long as you wear that Bajoran uniform, we're allies," the offender said with his lips peeled back. "Make sure you never take it off."

He nodded to his companion and the two of them stalked off.

Odo remained unimpressed, either by the Klingons or by himself. He hadn't scared them off. They'd deliberately kept control of themselves. Why?

"I didn't know you spoke Klingon," he said to Garak as he watched the Klingons round the curve of the Promenade's wide corridor.

"You'd be surprised," Garak said, "at the kind of things you can learn while you're doing alterations."

Garak entered his shop and wished he could find a nonsuspicious reason for keeping it closed. That would be too much of a signal. Everyone would be on him with questions to which he had no proper answers. Sisko would have questions, Odo would, the Klingons would have questions, everyone would.

There should be some kind of personal security measures in here. Something keyed to his own hand or eye or blood. Something that he could activate with brain waves. Any garden-variety master spy could fabricate such a system—what a challenge it would be to come up with something that even Odo couldn't turn into a key and breach.

Now Garak had a new hobby—figuring out a security system that Odo couldn't turn into himself. Was there anything Odo couldn't turn into? Hmmm . . . a raindrop?

On the other hand, there were times like these, when Garak would attract just as much attention by leaving his security measures off, thereby letting Drex and friends know they were expected back. Decisions, decisions.

He reached out to move a rack of nightdresses, and on the periphery of his vision someone moved to his left. A moment later there was also motion to his right.

They were here already. Five minutes earlier than expected. Maybe he had said two words too many.

How damned predictable they were. *Probably taught at the age of three—it's part of being a Klingon . . . beat up a lot of people and always do the most predictable thing.*

He swung around and pretended to be surprised. Four Klingons blocked his exit, including the two he and Odo had met on the Promenade. Drex and Ruktah.

They were exceptionally angry. Humiliated, most likely, on finding out that he had understood what they had said when they were in his shop before.

He had counted on that. It was what brought them back here now. They would vent their insult and wring the information out of him that they had left without before.

Garak controlled his facial expression with effort. He made his eyes gleam and his lips spread thin in what might have been taken as a smile. They were here, where he wanted them. He couldn't possibly stop what was about to happen. It was the price to be paid. If he showed fear, he would be even worse off.

"Let me guess," he said. "You're either lost, or you're desperately searching for a good tailor."

Drex wasn't tickled, any more than he had been when Garak had teased him on the Promenade by understanding his crack about Odo's mother not letting the constable speak to men. That had been the bait, after all—humiliate them, and they will follow you anywhere.

Drex stepped forward and landed a slaughtering punch to the tailor's midsection.

Explosive pain bolted through Garak—he was surprised at how much it hurt. His lungs crumpled. His knees buckled under him.

As Garak slid back and the other Klingons closed in, Drex flexed his gloved fists.

"Guess again."

The gloves were studded. Not just the punch, but the impact of the studs crashed into Garak's ribs and drove him violently backward. He slammed against the computer console, then folded forward over blinding pain, his lungs screaming for air and his vision bursting with lights.

Before those lights faded, they hit him again.

"Give us the access to the memory banks, Cardassian," Ruktah demanded.

Gasping as he hung over the shoe rack, Garak choked, "You . . . wouldn't . . . appreciate it."

Clamped fists came down on his shoulder like a sledgehammer. He felt the bone crack and heard the sound of it in the ear on that side. The force of the blow drove him to the floor on his face. The taste of blood filled his mouth.

Drex dragged him to his feet and held him on his toes. "Give it up, Cardassian."

Feeling his head fall back on his broken shoulder blade, Garak wheezed, "Sorry. You'll have to get it yourself . . . this is a self-serve establishment now. By the way . . . I'm relatively sure my mother can take you."

"Swine!" Drex bellowed, and laid into Garak's ribs again with punishing efficiency.

It was working. The more Garak insisted he knew nothing, the more they were sure he knew everything. Predictable. He didn't dare hand over what they wanted. Being typical Klingons, they would figure that if he gave it to them, it wasn't worth anything. Any minute now they would—

Drex pitched Garak backward into Ruktah's unkind grip and growled, "I will take it somehow!"

He plunged to the computer console and hammered it as if it were Garak's shoulders. Right on time.

Slamming his fist to the board, Drex roared, "It's got a retina lock on it! We could've had it anytime! Bring me his head!"

"Please," Garak gargled, "bring the rest of me also. . . ."

Ruktah dragged him to the board and smashed his face up against the reader screen. It flashed red light in his eye, then whistled and downloaded file after file into the terminal cartridge.

"Hah!" Drex bolted. "It's ours!"

"Then get it and let's go," Ruktah said.

He hoisted Garak a foot in the air, then threw him like a ball into the bulkhead.

When Garak slid to the deck, Ruktah kicked him in the legs with those big hard-toed boots. "Can I kill this one now?"

"Leave him on his floor." Drex snatched the cartridge and stuffed it somewhere in his plates of armor. "Better he lie in his own drool than have a good death."

"But he'll tell them we took it!"

"Who cares?" Drex enjoyed one more kick at Garak's legs as he lay helpless and gasping. "His foul Cardassian mouth tells no truths. No one will believe him. Better leave him alive to confuse them."

"I hate you," Ruktah gnashed, and spit on Drex.

"And I hate you," Drex said. "So what? Let's go."

CHAPTER
5

"GARAK . . . GARAK . . . take it easy. . . ."

Very deep voice, pounding through his head, which was already pounding quite well on its own.

Blur of clothing on the rack above, hanging crookedly now. The collapsed shoe rack. Shoes all over the floor in front of his face.

He was lying on his side. Tilting. Wall shifting angles. Someone was turning him over. There were echoes in the shop.

"Garak, you all right?"

"I'm . . ." Blood gurgled in his throat. The attempt to speak was followed by a raft of moans. He couldn't get a whole breath.

"You're safe now. Take it easy."

That wasn't an echo. It was Sisko's deep voice.

These were Sisko's big hands gripping his arm, pulling him ever so slowly to a sitting position.

"You'll be able to breathe better now." Sisko's face wobbled beside him. He was pulling Garak up against a crate of waistbands. "What happened to you?"

"Klingons came in," Garak gulped and gritted his teeth against the pain in his ribs. "Acted very rudely. . . . They wanted . . . patterns for the . . . latest pajamas. Naturally, I refused."

Sisko steadied him with a hand on his broken shoulder, and with the other hand held a cotton blouse to Garak's bleeding face.

"I'll bet," he scolded. He nodded up at the console. "They accessed your computer. Why?"

"They didn't tell me, Captain. Whatever they stole, I'm sure it was . . . information I just happened to put in this morning. Isn't that a . . . coincidence?"

Crushing an arm across his tortured ribs, Garak eyed Sisko. They had a somewhat elastic relationship, but it was definitely a relationship. A foggily defined alliance. Garak lived here on *Deep Space Nine,* and Sisko protected him. In return, Garak sometimes protected Sisko and *Deep Space Nine.* He wouldn't tell Sisko everything, but . . .

"What did they look like?" the captain asked. "What were they wearing?"

"Tall . . . wide . . . the usual . . . I couldn't quite get a look at them."

"You couldn't. Why not?"

"Because," Garak managed, one shattered breath at a time, "if I knew who they were, I'd be . . . obliged to press charges. It's better for all of us if they . . . go back to their ship, and take with them whatever they took from me. Now they'll leave us alone. Don't worry, Captain . . . they didn't get anything of any importance."

Sisko watched him cannily and almost smiled. Almost.

"Garak," he said, "sometimes I don't know whether to shake your hand or have you shot."

Garak nodded, then winced. "Either . . . would hurt right now."

Gingerly Sisko patted him on the arm. "The doctor is on his way."

"I can't believe you're not pressing charges."

Pain throbbed through Garak's back, thighs, and ribs, but he tried to offer a shrug to the doctor's comment. There were two or three muscles left in his right shoulder, enough to manage that.

"Constable Odo and Captain Sisko expressed similar concern," he said as Bashir picked and tapped at him with instruments of healing. "But really, Doctor, there was no harm done."

Julian Bashir stood back and looked him in the face. "They broke seven of your transverse ribs and fractured your clavicle."

Unexpectedly, Garak felt bad at the doctor's concern, for that was what lay beneath the clinical readout. Not just what damage the Klingons had done, but that they had done it at all. And would they come back, perhaps to do worse next time? Bashir was Garak's closest friend on this station. He took Garak at face value, without the haze of suspicion that kept most others at arm's length.

Hoping to ease the worry, Garak offered him a

mollifying grin. "But I got off several cutting remarks that no doubt did serious damage to their egos."

"Garak, it's not funny."

"I'm serious, Doctor. Thanks to your ministrations, I'm almost completely healed. The damage I did to them will last a lifetime." He paused for a moment's enjoyment of Klingon psychological thinness, then continued in a calculated way. "What I can't understand is their inexplicable hostility toward me. Maligning Constable Odo is one thing. After all, he's a changeling and the Klingons don't know him as well as we do. But relations between the Klingon and Cardassian Empires have never been anything but amicable."

"With the exception of the Betreka Nebula incident," Bashir said, putting unexplained pressure on Garak's left shoulder, then adding the talents of a hypospray.

"A minor skirmish," Garak downplayed.

He knew he was stretching the use of that phrase, but didn't feel like searching out another one. The Cardassians were bombastic, hungry for power, the Klingons irate and greedy. The mixture was no good. So far, though, because each was timid to face down the Federation, conditions between them had remained stable.

"That minor skirmish lasted eighteen years," the doctor pointed out.

Garak shook his head. "That was ages ago. Maybe they decided they just didn't like me."

The doctor smirked. "Not like you? Impossible."

"You're right, as always, Doctor," Garak tossed off. "They must've mistaken me for someone else."

Bashir was gazing at him. Garak knew he wasn't fooling the doctor, that his surface lies were easily taken as lies and that he had come, in the company of these people, to expect to be read so. They knew him better than anyone ever had, though he had deliberately protected them from his clouded past.

Still, he had enjoyed being one of them for the past few years. They had defended him without really comprehending who it was they were defending. Bashir and the others, Sisko, Kira—they didn't make demands or require him to come clean about his past before they would be on his side in the present. They were decent people.

He had come to appreciate that.

"Garak," Bashir said, "I want you to talk to Captain Sisko about some private protection. After all, that's one of the benefits of living on a station run by Starfleet."

Garak looked up at him. "You mean, a bodyguard?"

"Yes, of course. I'm sure they can spare one Security man to escort you about for a few days."

"I'm sure that's not necessary, Doctor. They'll probably be leaving soon."

"Really?" Bashir tipped his head and drew his brow. "What makes you say a thing like that?"

"You know Klingons," Garak offered vaguely. "No attention span."

"I have it."

"Bring it to me."

Martok reached out to Drex as his second plowed back onto the bridge of the *Negh'Var,* and took from him the computer cartridge that had come perhaps a bit too easily.

"Did you get this from the Cardassian?" he asked.

"Yes," Drex said. "He is a coward and a worm."

"Did you kill him?"

"No."

"Did he give you the information or did you take it from him? Tell me that."

As Martok put the cartridge into their engineering computer access port and battled with it to override the Federation codes, Drex said, "No, General. He refused to give it. We beat him and threatened him, but he held back from us."

"Then how did you get it?"

"The computer had only a retina lock. We pushed his face into it."

"I see." Martok thought about that, then nodded. "Better. If he had given it to you, I would take it as all fabrications. Let us see what we are up against."

Together they watched as the United Federation of Planets crest rolled across the screen, then several skeletal graphics of the station of *Deep Space Nine,* and finally the information they were looking for.

Martok murmured as the pictures scanned by on the screen. "Standard phaser sail towers . . . upper and lower emitter stations covering hundred-and-twenty-degree segments of space . . . no recent upgrades . . . some use of shadow photons to give the impression of strength. Called 'Quaker guns,' the images are named after logs used in forts on Earth, made to look like cannons, to fool the enemy."

"Yes," Drex said. "I heard DS9 had used those photon shadows before."

Martok nodded and continued murmuring as the schematics rolled before them. "Structural tower and deflector screens with standard outer shield wall, no new technology . . . six fusion reactors, only two working . . . attitude-control thrusters a bit rusty, in need of some maintenance . . . current engineer Chief Tam O'Shanter reporting."

The scrolling ended, and the screen went to simple green.

The general sat back in the engineer's chair and sighed a great sigh. "So, this station is still almost as toothless as when the Cardassians had it."

"Yes," Drex said, and Martok noticed that his second-in-command was plied with relief that his information had turned out to be useful, his mission an apparent success. "According to this, Starfleet hasn't had time or resources to increase the armament here."

"The station was never meant to defend itself," Martok told him. "When the Cardassians had it, they kept it surrounded with ships that handled its defense."

"And all Sisko has to defend himself are Quaker guns. They simply *look* like they're heavily armed." He reached out and patted the computer screen like a pet. "Now I know not to believe the photon shadows I see here. All they have is that one ship docked on the lower pylon, and we can handle one ship. Drex, I am fully satisfied. *Deep Space Nine* is no threat to us."

"General," his helm officer interrupted, "pardon this—there is a ship leaving from the station. The freighter *Xhosa*. You mentioned it before—"

"Yes," Martok said, and hoisted to his feet. "Contact Commander Kaybok on the outer perimeter of the fleet, scrambled frequency."

"Yes, General . . . Commander Kaybok standing by."

"Put him on."

"Kaybok."

"Kaybok, your parade is beginning. Aren't you watching?"

"Yes—yes, I see the freighter. I will follow them under cloak."

"When you're far out, stop them and pretend to search."

"Pretend? I thought—"

"Yes, but I have a better idea. We cannot find changelings with blood tests. How can we give a blood test to a wall or a chair? Besides, I don't want any ship coming and going from Cardassian space. How will we know who comes and goes with them?"

"Then what should I do?"

"I want you to go ahead with the search, and while this search is going on I want you to place an explosive on board that vessel. Stop it, search it, apologize, leave, and an hour later it explodes. No one will ever know."

CHAPTER
6

"SHIP APPROACHING, KASIDY."

"What'd you say, Wayne?"

"I said we've got some kind of a ship approaching. I can't read it very well for some reason, but I'm picking it up on the energy-flux meters."

"Are they hailing us?"

"I guess you could take this as a hail. But when I gave them a flash-response, they didn't come back."

"All right, I'm coming up."

Her hand smeared with lubricant from underneath the floor panels, Kasidy Yates used one wrist to shove back a flop of her hair as she climbed out of the lower thruster access vault. She came up two short companionways through the arteries of her heavily loaded freighter and onto her bridge.

Her jumpsuit was smeared with lubricant, so she

used it to wipe her hands. First Mate Wayne Sheppard was huddled over the main sensors as she approached him and looked over his red hair at the monitors.

"I don't get it," he said. "I know there's a ship out there. Look at this movement. And there's another one. That's a warp shift. Wouldn't you say that's what it is?"

"Definitely not natural phenomenon," she murmured, blinking into the screen. "Boy, this screen is bright. After this run, I'm going to put in for maintenance and have about half the systems on this ship overhauled."

"I hope that includes the showers," Wayne said distractedly. "There it is again. Now, that can't be anything but a vessel!"

Kasidy gripped him hard by the shoulders. "Energy flux . . . that's a cloak! Wayne, it's a cloak! Luis! Cindy! B.J.! On deck! Trouble! Wayne, evasive maneuvers!"

"Evasive! You've gotta be kidding!"

Kasidy dodged to the helm and took it herself. "What's our current speed?"

Wayne slid into the nav seat beside her. "Two point five."

"I'm going to warp four."

"Kasidy—"

"We've gotta try, Wayne."

"Right, okay."

"Screen on. Power up defense."

"I don't even know if it's hooked up."

"Luis! Where is he?"

"I'm down here."

"Have we got weapons?"

"A couple."

"Fire 'em up!"

"Well . . . yeah, awright. Just a minute."

Wayne leaned into the nav board and tried to hold the big old ship together as they went to warp four faster than was safe. "I told you this Cardassian run was risky, Kas."

"Gotta make a living," she muttered back at him as she kept her eyes on the main screen. "But I don't think this is Cardassians . . . look at that exhaust mixture. Can you identify that?"

"Trying . . ."

"Put our shields up too." Suddenly Kasidy drew a quick breath and held it. "What am I thinking! Cloaks! DS9!"

Wayne looked at her. "What? What?"

"Klingons, that's what!"

"That's crazy! What do they want from us way out here? What do they want from us at all?"

"Doesn't matter." She leaned into the helm controls. "Get the shields up. Let's make for the Cardassian border. Maybe they won't cross it."

"Sure," Wayne grunted. "And Tellarites don't stink."

"Decloak now."

"Decloaking, Commander."

"Come around in front of them. Cut them off and force them to reduce speed."

Kaybok knew his way around pursuing and stopping other vessels. It was his best thing. He had come up through the ranks as a border-patrol guard and there was still the hunter in him. A freighter could not even in its dreams hope to outrun a Bird-of-Prey.

They were trying, though. He was tempted to reduce speed, just to elongate the chase. But how would that look in his command log? Better it show that he took the freighter quickly. After all, it was only a freighter.

Quite a big vessel, that hulk, he saw as they came up on it and veered around in front.

"Shall I fire on them?" his second-in-command asked.

"No," Kaybok said. "They'll stand down."

"They're turning again."

"Turn with them."

This was hardly a contest. The ships were so vastly different from each other that they had completely different advantages and there was no match between them in any way. Lacking in speed, firepower, and maneuverability, the freighter was already staggering before them. However, if the Bird-of-Prey ever needed to carry fifty thousand tons of atmosphere-controlled cargo, it would likely falter too.

Kaybok smiled. "Keep forcing them to turn until they go in circles."

His second nodded, then passed the order of specific maneuvers to their helm officer.

"They're reducing speed," his science officer reported from over his left shoulder. "Falling out of hyperlight."

"Fall out also," Kaybok said. "Come around to their bow and stand fast."

On the screen before them it appeared the gnarled freighter was coming around to face them, but of course it was the opposite. In a moment, all movement sagged to a stop. He looked down the big ship's nostrils for a few satisfied seconds.

"Hail them," he said.

"Hailing. Response coming in."

"Put it through, audio."

"This is the captain of the Xhosa. *You're blocking our passage. Do you have an explanation?"*

A woman.

Kaybok waited to see if she would get nervous and ask more questions, but she didn't. She was waiting for his response. She probably was the captain, then.

"We are the border guard," he said.

"This isn't your border. This is the Cardassian-Bajoran border, and since you mention it, we're not even there yet."

"You are crossing into hostile space."

"We have a Starfleet merchant permit to cross into Cardassian space. You have absolutely no jurisdiction here. I'm putting a call through to Starfleet right now. You'd better back off and let us pass."

Kaybok glanced at his second. "Scramble that signal."

"Attempting."

"Xhosa," he began again, "drop your shields. We intend to search your vessel."

"Search? For what? My cargo is completely legal! You have no permission to occupy any vessel!"

She sounded indignant. A typical merchant captain.

"Federation legality means nothing to me," he told her. "Orders from our fleet commander and my guns give me permission. Drop your shields or there will be weapons fired."

The woman became silent. For nearly one minute there was no answer from her. Kaybok was willing to wait. He could smash her engines now, or ten minutes from now. Either way there would be cooperation.

"All right. Don't fire. You can search."

The woman's voice was tentative, but the words were right. She was sensible.

"Lower your shields," Kaybok said. "Our landing party will come aboard in four minutes. End communication."

He stood up and swung to his second-in-command. "You lead the boarding party. Take the explosive with you and install it in their engine room. Make sure none of them see you do this. Set the timer just before you leave their ship."

"I understand what to do."

"Take twelve crewmen."

"Twelve? Three-quarters of our crew?"

"You must effect a convincing search. It will take many men to rustle their crew into place, saturate their decks, distract them enough to install the bomb. Don't look at me like that, Onnak."

The second didn't care for taking such a large portion of their crew to a foreign vessel, but a few well-placed glowers from Kaybok put him down. This had to be staged well, or the wrong thing would happen. If the captain and crew of this freighter figured out what Kaybok was up to, then Kaybok would have to destroy them here and now instead of by remote, and there would be evidence.

As he watched Onnak disappear into the lift, heading to the transport pad, he thought about destroying the freighter now. Then there would be no doubt of any changelings going from here to there on that ship.

But Martok had other ideas. Martok might be afraid to stand up to the Federation. Kaybok couldn't tell. Kaybok didn't care.

"Kasidy . . ."

"I see it. Just keep your eyes on their transport-beam indicators, Wayne. I want to know the instant they start to transport."

"You sure you can do this?"

"No, but Klingons are cocky. They don't put safeties on their equipment. I think we can do it. Luis? Can you hear me down there?"

A voice threaded out of the wide companionway to the engine room. "Yeah, I can."

"Keep the engines warm . . . don't let the warp core drop its temperature or they'll pick up the change when we fire it up again."

"Gotcha."

"And stay away from the core or you'll get burned. I'm keeping my finger on the emergency warp button. Be ready to compensate."

"We're ready down here, Kas."

The plaintive call of her engineer from down inside the companionway was all the reassurance she would get right now.

"And, Wayne, as soon as we break away from their

damping field, I want a message put through to *Deep Space Nine*. The Klingons'll be on us in ten seconds. That's all the time you'll have. Be sure to include our location. If we're going to have any help, they've got to know where to find us."

"I'm ready if you're ready—Kas, I'm reading a transporter wave! They're coming!"

Kasidy tensed over the emergency warp button and held her breath—

Just as she began to hear the irritating buzz of a transporter beam, and just as she saw the faint beginnings of the glow of reintegrating matter, she pressed the button and shouted to her crew.

"Shields up! Emergency warp, now!"

"Reverse transport! Reverse! Reverse!"

Kaybok shouted and struck out at the face of his helm officer, knocking the man aside to reach the communication pad that would tie him through to his transporter platform.

On the main viewscreen, the freighter became smaller and smaller as it bolted into emergency warp speed and was suddenly light-days off.

"Get them back! Pull them back!"

He shouted into the comm unit. Though he was staring at the empty space that a moment ago housed the freighter, he was screaming at his transporter officer. His fingers clawed into the cushioning rubber of the helm console's edge. He gritted his teeth. His breath came and went, came and went. His brain screamed.

Silence enfolded them, all but the subtle whirr of systems on his bridge and the faint dimming of lights as the ship went into high effort to choke back its transporter beam.

He stared at the screen. Empty now.

Sucking a lungful, he gasped, "Transport! Did you get them back?"

The open comm line crackled. He heard a shuffle come through the system. Muffled voices.

"Transport! Answer me!"

"Commander . . ."

"Yes! Answer!"

"Sir . . . we got them back . . ."

"In what condition?"

"Sir . . . they were in open space . . ."

Kaybok's face twisted in agony. He demanded again, "What is their condition?"

"They are . . . they are frozen, sir. Suffocated."

Twelve members of his crew. Twelve trained space warriors, wasted by a woman's trick.

He felt as if his skull were being crushed, his chest collapsing.

Twelve.

He reached down with his giant hand and caught the beard of his helm officer and dragged him that way back to the ship's steering mechanism.

"Catch them," Kaybok chafed. His teeth went together and his lips peeled back. "Catch that ship. Catch it now. Catch it."

"I don't like this."

"I know you don't."

"Nothing in this galaxy can make me trust them. I've never trusted them," Kira said.

"I understand that," Sisko answered calmly.

"Alliance is just a convenient word to get them whatever they wanted. They're just Cardassians in sheep's clothing when they talk peace."

"You're probably right."

"If they want to be allies with us and stand with us against the Dominion, then why aren't they being upfront about the numbers of their personnel here?"

"Can't you count Klingons, Major?"

"Yes, sir, of course I can count them, but they refuse to give any identification when they come on and off the station and they also refuse to wear comm badges, so there's no good way to tell if the same ones are coming back and forth or if they're different ones. They all look the same to me."

"Something wrong, Major? You look uncomfortable."

"Oh . . . I'm sorry, sir, it's just that Dax took me into one of those Trill supersensual bathhouse holosuite programs and I think I got a little too much steam. I'm a little raw."

Ben Sisko raised a brow at Major Kira as they both slouched in their chairs across his desk from one another. "For pity's sake, don't tell me where."

Kira was hunch-shouldered and gripping the ends of the chair's arms with her fingertips as if hanging on at high speed. Her short auburn hair caught the reading lamplight that pinked her complexion. Sisko knew how she felt—out of control. Not with the Trill program, but with everything else going on aboard *Deep Space Nine.* There were Klingons everywhere, not behaving as if they belonged or wanted to be here, but not providing any reason for Sisko to pitch them off.

"And that incident with Garak this morning bothers me," Kira said. "Why would Klingons gang up on him in his shop and use him for a punching bag?"

Sisko gazed at her. "If you were a Klingon, wouldn't you hit Garak?"

"Apparently he and Odo had a confrontation with these criminals on the Promenade, and I guess they didn't want to take on Odo, so they settled for Garak."

"He'll be all right, Major."

"Yes, I know. In his twisted way I think he enjoyed the attention. Assault is a reason to ask them to stay on board their ships or at least to limit the numbers in the boarding parties."

"It would be . . . but he's not pressing charges."

Kira pondered, "Why would Garak avoid pressing charges against Klingons? He doesn't have any particular attachment to them." She'd made the statement, and now found herself flicking the idea back at Sisko. "Does he?"

Her large eyes, supremely feminine in spite of the hardness they perpetually carried, widened.

Sisko shrugged. "Garak? Who knows? We haven't had two straight answers from him in the whole time he's been on *Deep Space Nine*. What's the status of the task force? Do we have a vessel count yet?"

"The Klingon ships keep cloaking and decloaking, so it's impossible to get an exact count. But so far, we've been able to identify at least twenty different warships in the vicinity of the station."

When Sisko was about to make an unpleasant response, the comm chirped and cut him off. It always seemed to know exactly when to blip. Just before a kiss or just before he was about to say something he'd regret.

"Captain," Dax's voice came through, *"we're receiving a priority one distress call from the freighter* Xhosa."

Kira came out of her slump. "Kasidy's ship?"

"She left the station an hour ago," Sisko said. "Dax, put her through."

He turned to his monitor just as a close-up of Kasidy Yates crackled up on the screen, centered on the bridge of her freighter. Her brow was creased with worry.

"This is the freighter Xhosa *to Deep Space Nine. We're under attack by—"*

The image sliced off cleanly, leaving only static. Cut off at the source.

Shoving to his feet, Sisko dodged for the Ops door. "Come on," he called to Kira, but she was already there.

Ops was a clutch of tight shoulders and intense eyes, in the center of which was Dax, picking at the main table, trying to draw that signal back in.

"Her signal's been jammed," she said immediately.

"Get me a fix on her location," Sisko said. "Then tell the crew of the *Defiant* to man their stations." He swung toward the turbolift, motioning Kira after him. "We'll meet you on the bridge."

"Forward scanners are detecting the *Xhosa* at bearing zero-one-seven mark three-four-six."

Dax's report was sham reassurance to Ben Sisko as he reposed in his command chair. The frustration of being so far away when Kasidy needed help was offset surprisingly by the mobility of having a ship. For years as commander of DS9 he had nothing to match the *Defiant*. He had the powerful little runabouts, but they weren't long-range battleships like this one. This ship, heavy and double-plated, armed at every quarter, was a tough muscle of a vessel for a tough region of open space.

When he had wrangled permission to bring *Defiant* to DS9, he had accepted the "temporary" clause in the ship's assignment, but he had never intended to give her back to Starfleet Command.

Fortunately, they accepted this outpost as the ship's permanent dockage.

The battleship changed the whole tenor of the sector, and of Sisko's status. Instead of being the commander of a distant outpost, he became the custodian of the entire sector, for now he was mobile. Crimes committed in deep space and even acts of war could now expect immediate response from Sisko himself, and he had the might to back up the laws imposed out here.

He liked that.

Even now he was speeding toward Kasidy's ship instead of being trapped on DS9 waiting for Starfleet to dispatch somebody from way over there to get way over here.

"I'm here," he murmured as he stared at the black silk of outer space on the main screen, and the endless stars. They were up to full warp, and bits of space debris shot past them, making bright white and yellow brushstrokes on space.

At the weapons console, Kira stiffened. "I'm picking up another ship nearby. They've got *Xhosa* in a tractor beam."

Sisko sat up a little straighter. "On screen."

The screen changed without a flicker, as if hungry to show them what it saw.

A demonic Bird-of-Prey hung over Kasidy Yates's bulky freighter, not alongside but with its forward weapons arrays pointed right at the ship in unconcealed threat.

"A Klingon ship!" Kira burst out. Was she really that surprised?

"I can't get through to *Xhosa,*" Dax said. "They must still be jamming her communications."

Sisko set his jaw. "Hail the Klingon vessel."

Working quickly, Dax frowned over her controls. She was having trouble. There was some kind of resistance from the other ship. Sisko didn't prod. She'd get it in a minute.

Surely the Klingons has picked up their approach and had read what kind of vehicle was coming at them. *Defiant* was her own kind of message.

The screen blipped again, and on it was a particularly unattractive Klingon—but Kira was right about that. Who could tell?

"This is Commander Kaybok of the M'Char. *What is it you want?"*

"I want to know why you stopped that ship," Sisko said bluntly, without identifying himself or his ship. They probably knew already.

"We have orders to search all vessels attempting to leave Bajoran space."

Kira squared her shoulders. "Search them for what?"

"For shapeshifters. Each ship will be scanned, its cargo searched, and the crew members and passengers subjected to genetic testing."

"On whose authority?" Sisko asked, holding back from telling them that he was the only person who could order anything like that in this sector.

"On the authority of Chancellor Gowron and the Klingon High Council."

"The Klingon High Council has no jurisdiction over ships in Bajoran space."

A glitch—he'd almost said "in my space." He realized it would've been a tiny error, but somehow just thinking it invigorated him. It *was* his space.

Kaybok looked—maybe jealous? Certainly angry. He was hot-faced and tense. Kasidy must've put up a fight.

The Klingon seemed to want to snap something, but visibly controlled himself. Yes, he did know who Sisko was. After a few moments he decided to say, *"We assumed you would welcome our assistance."*

Measuring the Klingon's attitude, Sisko thought better of flexing his authority again. That wasn't enough of a reason for Kaybok to stop these searches. After Sisko left, he would keep doing it. Of course, he hadn't stopped yet.

"Do you have any evidence that there are changelings aboard this particular ship?" he asked.

Kaybok glowered. He knew he was being cornered. *"How can we have evidence until we have conducted our tests?"*

"Commander," Kira spoke up, "Bajoran law strictly prohibits the unwarranted search and seizure of vessels in our territory."

"I have my orders," Kaybok slung back, and cut off his transmission.

Robbed of its source, the screen went back to a picture of the two ships.

"The Klingon ship has increased power to its tractor beam," Dax reported, glancing from the screen to her controls, then back again. "It looks like they're preparing to board the *Xhosa.*"

"Major," Sisko began, "raise shields and power up the forward phasers. See if that gets their attention."

Kira moved her hands across her panel. "Shields up. Forward phasers standing by."

Pressing her lips into a line, Dax said, "They're still not releasing the tractor beam."

Sisko pressed back against his chair. "Fire a warning shot two hundred meters off their starboard bow."

Kira turned and looked at him. She would rather launch a direct hit, he knew. But that wouldn't answer any of her questions, would it?

"Yes, sir," she said, and pressed the firing mechanism.

Defiant's high-powered phasers discharged across the black veldt, creasing open space with a near-blinding light.

Dax buried a grin. "Commander Kaybok would like to speak to you."

"Let's hear what he has to say."

The screen changed again.

"Captain, this is outrageous!"

"I agree," Sisko acknowledged. "But you're not leaving me much choice. You're in violation of Bajoran law. Now, I'll ask you one more time . . . release that ship immediately."

"We are your allies!"

"Major, lock phasers on the *M'Char*'s engines. Prepare to fire on my command."

This wasn't just any ship—it was Kasidy's ship. He wouldn't let these bullies push anybody around, but having the chance to defend Kasidy gave him a sense of being the knight in shining armor. She was going to see him dare the Klingons to knock the chip off his shoulder—it embarrassed him a little that he enjoyed that. He felt like a schoolboy playing with the biggest toy in the galaxy.

A little louder than necessary, Kira said, "Phasers ready."

Kaybok stared splinters at them over the screen. He looked about ready to blow his brow ridge off. Twisting to one of his officers, he growled something in Klingon about the tractor beam. On Dax's board, the sensor light indicating active traction abruptly clicked off.

Turning to face Sisko again, Kaybok said, "Gowron will hear of this!"

The transmission snapped off again, and again they were looking at the two ships. *Xhosa* was now floating free, and a moment later the Klingon ship tipped its wing and bore off. Soon they were at high speed, and soon they were gone.

"I'm receiving a hail from the *Xhosa*," Dax reported. "It's Captain Yates."

"Captain," she said, her voice thready with relief, *"I don't know what you said to those Klingons, but it must've been good."*

That was her way of telling him how determined the Klingons had been and how she had no doubts they would've made good on their threat of genetic testing. Sisko guessed Yates might have offered to turn back to DS9 and the Klingons had refused even that.

Or had she pulled some trick on them that made them finally throw that tractor beam on her? Why were they so interested in her ship?

"Is everyone all right?" he asked her.

She broke into a smile. "Everyone is fine."

"I'm glad to hear that."

They fell into silence, communicating with the gaze of gathering affection and the undertone of personal meaning. Sisko felt his expression give away how much he wished he could go with her, and that there wouldn't be so many days before they saw each other again. Around him, his crew pretended not to notice, but they were bad liars.

"We'll keep you on sensors as long as possible. But I doubt the Klingons will give you any more trouble."

"I appreciate that, Captain. I'll see you in about two weeks."

He held back his smile, but it showed. He could feel it. "You know where to find me."

"General!"

Kaybok jolted to his feet at the gasp of his bridge's

turbolift doors. The light from inside the lift was almost blocked off by the mass of Martok and six other fleet commanders as the group spewed out of the small space.

"Kaybok," Martok began. Such a tone.

The fleet commanders spread across Kaybok's bridge. All remained silent. He stared from one to the next. No charity there.

"General—" he began.

"Stand there!" Martok cut him off.

Kaybok stood straight, his hands icy at his sides.

"Did you board the freighter *Xhosa?*" Martok began evenly, suddenly lowering his voice.

Now Kaybok's feet were cold too. "I . . . I . . . I stopped it, General—"

"But you did not board it?"

"They . . . put up their shields, General!"

Martok paced in front of him. "And their shields stopped you?"

"No, sir—"

"Then there is an explosive aboard."

"No—no, sir."

Martok paced around behind him. "Who stopped you from this?"

"It was Sisko! He came in his battle barge! I didn't know if it was part of your plan to fire on a Starfleet ship."

"No, it's not part of my plan yet. How did Sisko know you were heading off the freighter? Did you not have sense enough to block its transmission?"

"Of course, General. They got away from me . . . for a few seconds."

"And when you caught them again, why did you not board?"

Shuddering under the general's interrogation, Kaybok realized there was no way out of the funnel into which he had fallen. The sentence had to be said.

"I had not . . . enough crew."

Martok paused in front of him. "Yes. And where is your crew, Kaybok?"

Almost hesitating again, Kaybok realized his hesitation itself was a grave error. He looked around at the other fleet commanders and finally back to Martok.

Flatly he confessed, "They were killed."

Martok stopped pacing. "When you beamed them into open space?"

The bridge seemed to spin. "Yes."

Turning away, Martok was a ball of rage. "Execute him."

The most senior fleet commander came forward and plucked from Kaybok's belt his family's ceremonial dagger.

Kaybok held out a hand. "General—"

Martok swung about. "Do not beg!"

Stunned silent, Kaybok stood there with his mouth open.

A hard force struck him in the middle of his back. He realized he had been looking at Martok and not paying attention to the fleet commander who had taken his dagger.

That fleet commander—it was Paghal. The two of them had served together in their first ship. They had been scarcely children, so eager to see space, to venture together and come back with stories and songs. . . .

As the strength drained from his legs and his lungs collapsed within his chest, Kaybok turned slowly to look into the face of his earlier companion.

Strange. Paghal seemed not to remember.

CHAPTER
7

"I STEPPED OVER him like the old fool he was."

Martok sat in his command chair on the bridge of the *Negh'Var* and used Kaybok's own ceremonial dagger to chip Kaybok's blood from his boots. He found a particular poetry in doing that.

"Things are falling apart here, Chancellor. It is my recommendation that we dispense with *Deep Space Nine* and get on with our plans. If we are to attack Cardassia, then let us attack Cardassia. And for any who stand in our path, let us kick them out of the way."

The monitor before him, Chancellor of the High Council Gowron's hawklike blue eyes bore back at him, frosted by the interference caused by the scramble sequence of their communications system.

"You are moving too fast, General," Gowron said. *"We have information to gather before you strike."*

"I have much information already. I've confirmed that *Deep Space Nine* has virtually no weaponry."

"How did you do this?"

"I have sources on the station."

"Really . . ."

"I am ready to take the station."

"You are quick to shoot, Martok. There are other considerations."

"I have considered them. It will not work to pretend to be on shore leaves, then go out and pick at ships as they ramble by. I've found no advantage in coddling Starfleet. How long do you think they can be put off? If they fight," Martok said with a shrug, "then they fight. We have bigger enemies."

Gowron once had been as quick to wrestle as Martok felt now, but being chancellor had put forbearance in the other warrior's ways, and now, as war came upon them again, those ways were causing hesitations where there should be none. Martok was glad to be in his place as general of the fleet instead of chancellor of the High Council.

"Sisko will find us out soon," he said. "Already he has brought out his battleship once. He will figure out what we're doing, and he will bring Starfleet. I say we accept that. Let me take the station. The Founders will want to take it, and I want to take it first. It's the first line of defense of the wormhole. If the Dominion is to be stopped, it will be stopped here. *Deep Space Nine* should be a Klingon station!"

"They are still our allies." Gowron's face was bracketed in static as the chancellor sat back and shook his

head. *"I remind you, Martok, this is not just plunder for a handful of us. This is survival for all of us."*

"Chancellor," Martok persisted. "Accept the facts. When Sisko finds out what we're doing, the treaty will be over. Let me move the fleet away from this shell of a station and begin preparing to do what we came here to do."

True regret showed in Gowron's eyes.

After a moment he said, *"Very well. I will confer with the Council. Promise your fleet commanders that they will have a chance to defend against the coming enemy. We will do anything we have to do to keep the Dominion out of our quadrant. But for now, Starfleet has not betrayed us. We will not move against them until they do."*

"According to our long-range sensors, the Klingon task force has withdrawn to just outside Bajoran territory."

"So now they're in unclaimed space. And if they decide to continue searching ships . . ."

"There's nothing we can do about it."

Jadzia Dax spoke with practicality as she and Ben Sisko sat together in his office on DS9 as if none of the morning's activities had happened.

"Unless they try to stop a Federation or Bajoran vessel," she finished.

Sisko watched her, trying to find a hint of experience there that might tell him there was one thing he hadn't done, something he could yet do to divine the Klingons' motivations, but even Dax was uncharacteristically perplexed.

The comm line chirped as Sisko finished, "Which, so far, they haven't done."

"Captain," O'Brien's voice piped through, *"General Martok is here to see you."*

"Send him in."

Not entirely unexpected.

The door gasped, and Martok strode in with the posture of purpose stiffening his tall frame.

"General," Sisko began, "we need to talk about—"

"Sohk-vad!"

The Klingon plowed straight past Dax to the desk, and slammed a shining, angry, carved dagger in front of Sisko.

He swung around with such panache that his body armor jangled, and out he went.

Dax picked up the dagger and looked at what appeared to be a family crest.

"It's Commander Kaybok's," she said.

Sisko looked at it. "Why give it to me?"

"He's letting you know Kaybok is dead. Martok probably had him executed for disobeying orders."

Turning the knife in his hands, Sisko absorbed the grim news. Had Kaybok gone against Martok's wishes in cornering Kasidy's ship?

He doubted that. But other suspicions were confirmed. The Klingons were taking something very seriously, even to the point of risking the treaty with the Federation.

"Which means our next confrontation with the Klingons won't be resolved so easily. Any suggestions, old man?"

She shrugged with her eyes. "The longer the

Klingons stay here, the worse things are going to get. Whatever you're going to do, you'd better do it soon."

He thought about this for a few moments, wandering the thin lines separating the forces with which he had constantly to deal, and sought out one of the tricks that had given him advantage in sticky situations in the past.

He offered her a wry grin.

"Curzon told me once that in the long run the only people who can really handle Klingons are Klingons. Get me Starfleet Command."

CHAPTER
8

THE DAYS WERE long when there was no ship. Where there was no ship, there was no space, no risk, no reward or purpose. That unique entity which was more than vehicle, more than transportation, which somehow possessed life and reason beyond its designation as chamber of survival in an intolerable place—was gone for him.

Yes, there could be another ship. For all sailors through history who had lost a ship, there would always be another. Somehow, though, the hole remained empty. Nothing could take the place of the unique identity magically possessed by a good ship with a heart of oak. He hadn't yet gone looking for another.

Every sailor either knew that ship or wished for her,

the ship that had been slammed down hard but had picked herself up and brought her crew back in, safe. Every sailor understood that point when things changed between himself and the ship, when he found himself not only fighting to survive, but to bring the ship back because suddenly there had sprung to life a mutual loyalty.

And, of course, for so many there came that moment when one had to give up life for the other, and usually, as was right, the ship got the raw end of the deal.

Most ships would rather have it that way—die in a crash, in a ball of fire, at the bottom of a suffocating miasma, rather than wither in age, be converted to a barge, and eventually scrapped.

Thus the Galaxy-class *Starship Enterprise* had gotten the wish of ships. Crashed, and she had saved her crew doing it. Not a bad way to go.

Yet, to be one of those crew, one who had manned the bridge for so long . . . was a sorry fate.

This place, this planet of Boreth, was not unlike the landscape where the *Enterprise* had crash-landed. Veridian III. As forbidding as any world might become, given time. A fit place for a ship of exploration and battle to finally die.

I am a Klingon. Such thoughts of ship loyalty—this is a human thing, yet I feel it. I'm glad I feel it.

"Brother Worf?"

A cleric strode toward him, wearing the simple gathered robes of Boreth Monastery.

"Yes, Master Lourn?"

"I went below, to see if you were enjoying the

exercises, and you turn up here, watching from above. Why aren't you in the arena?"

Worf folded his hands and let them drop between his knees as he sat on his bench. Below them, in the wide open arena, two dozen Klingon men grappled and jousted in hand-to-hand combat exercises. The day's exercises weren't particularly fierce, but in the past hour there had been some blood drawn.

"This is my Silent Hour," Worf said evasively, hesitant to blurt out the truth.

"I thought you had already done two Silent Hours today," Lourn said. He didn't sit down.

"No . . . only one."

"And you chose to have a Silent Hour instead of participating below? I don't understand."

"I am having a Silent Hour," Worf fumed, raising his voice, "because I do not want to grapple, and Silence is my only other choice."

Lourn circled the small bench, one of several viewing benches settled up here on the promontory. "You sound hostile. Why don't you say the truth of why you do not go down?"

Worf peered at the scene below—other Klingons of his own age and ability grunting and grappling in bunches of threes and fours. Yesterday it had been twos and threes. Tomorrow it would be fours and fives. Next week it would be winners of the playoffs going one-to-one.

"It seems pointless," he finally said. He didn't feel like sparing Lourn's sensibilities. "Hand-to-hand combat . . . why do we bother? A child with a hand phaser could defeat the whole arena of muscles and blades. How often does such battle come up? There is more to life than this." He made a disapproving gesture. "This is not even how battle really is anymore. This is nothing but sport."

Lourn didn't come around or pace back and forth, but spoke from a fixed position behind him. "Battle will come more in your life. If it does not find you, you will go out and find it. This is our nature."

Worf bristled. "Are you saying that Klingons will go out into the galaxy and cause a conflict if none comes?"

"It is our nature," Lourn said again.

With a rough grunt, Worf said, "We should rise above such nature."

"That is your human upbringing talking."

Worf shifted on his bench just enough to see Lourn. "At this monastery you teach that conflict is inevitable, that rejecting it is rejecting reality, that species survive by being good at conflict. Planets orbit stars and intelligent beings will always conflict. But I have seen otherwise. Starfleet has shown me other wisdom."

Lourn made a sound that may have been a laugh. "How many times in Starfleet have you known it was time to strike a blow, and you were held back?"

Worf faced the arena again, troubled, angry. He had heard this ten times from Lourn just this week. He had no response to it. He didn't know the words to vocalize what the Federation wanted for the galaxy, yet he had seen it and he wanted it too.

"You're not alive because of wisdom, Worf," Lourn said evenly from behind him. "You're alive because of luck. Any gambling house knows, in the long run you cannot beat the odds. The coin may flip a thousand times to the same face, but if it is flipped enough times more, it will even out. It always does. Starfleet is made up of timid pacifists afraid to take a stand. Sooner or later they will hesitate to strike enough times that they will be destroyed."

"The Federation will stand its ground," Worf attempted, feeling his shoulders tremble with the effort of philosophical argument. He wasn't good at this. "I have seen them many times say, 'This is the line. Do not cross.'"

"Yet you don't understand where the line is, do you?" Lourn prodded. "You don't really know why they draw that line. You're a Klingon, Worf. You may never understand their line. You were raised by humans and of course you assumed some of their ways, but you're not a child anymore. You must cast aside the things your adoptive parents and their people were wrong about, that which is not you. You're having problems here because you're denying that you are Klingon."

Driven to fury by confusion, by his inability to verbalize what he believed, Worf spun around with his fist balled, aiming for the sound of Lourn's voice, planning to land a blow on that which he could not power down with words.

But Lourn wasn't there anymore. He had moved away, just back far enough that Worf's fist spun free and he struck at empty air, almost toppling himself from the bench.

"You see?" Lourn quietly said. "You're a Klingon

and I knew it. I knew what you would do. That blow you just missed is your true nature. By losing this argument, you have learned that you can't defend Starfleet because you don't understand it. You're a Klingon. You can't be human. The humans see things differently and that's why you don't know where they draw their lines. It's time for you to accept that and become fully Klingon. Worf . . . you are in the wrong place."

Haunted by his own prodigality, Worf gripped the edge of the bench. He wasn't angry at Lourn. The cleric was doing his job. Sifting Worf's identity and searching for clarity.

On the other hand, yes, he was angry at Lourn. Who could think such thoughts about the Federation, which had provided stability in the midst of galactic upheaval? Was that what it meant to be Klingon? To deny facts?

"Commander Worf!"

A third presence relieved him of having to speak to Lourn. He stood to his full height, towering over the newcoming Klingon by half a head as one of the monastery's clerks came toward them. "Yes, Brother Klasq?"

"I'm afraid we must interrupt your Silent Hour. Greetings, Master Lourn. Commander Worf, a communiqué has come for you. It's from Starfleet Command."

Worf glanced at Lourn. This was supposed to be his Silent Hour. It came twice a day, every day, rain, shine, hunger, storm, boredom, random thoughts, alien attack, planetary core explosion—nothing could stop it.

Except a communiqué from Starfleet Command. Right through the Silent Hour like a pincer.

Worf tried not to insult Brother Klasq, or satisfy Master Lourn, by plunging too quickly for the comm disk in the clerk's hand.

After all, there was no point in breaking bones.

CHAPTER
9

DEEP SPACE NINE. Ironically, not the ninth deep-space station established by the Federation. The "Nine" had something to do with the area of space—nine sectors, nine years trying to establish a post here, something like that. Worf hazily remembered the story, but had forgotten the reason.

It was good to once again wear his Starfleet uniform. Too long had he felt the robes of Boreth around his ankles, with Lourn constantly biting at those ankles. Too long had he lumbered about the monastery, discussing vagaries of life without pursuing life itself. Now it came to get him and he was glad for that.

But here?

It might as well be here. At least this would be a chance to avoid what Lourn had predicted for him. If he couldn't defeat his inner demons, perhaps he could avoid them.

Deep Space Nine was familiar enough, and still jaundiced in its way. The Cardassian architecture was annoying, as if it refused to forget who had built it. There was an air of simmering trouble here in these lava-gray halls with their structural arms arching overhead like the legs of a crouching spider.

Yes, here.

Worf shuffled from the docking pylon in a gaggle of other travelers just arriving, and a voice threaded to him over the grumble of conversation in the docking ring.

"Commander Worf!"

A ruddy face under buff curls appeared out of the crowd. Suddenly a touch of the *Enterprise* was back in his grip.

"Chief O'Brien," Worf greeted. "It has been a long time."

"Too long," O'Brien said. "Welcome aboard."

They strolled together through the crowd and into one of the lateral turbolifts that would take them through to the habitat ring, where the quarters were.

"I'll get you settled," O'Brien said. "How's the rest of the crew? The captain?"

"Captain Picard is well. As all commanders, he understood why he must lose his ship. The civilization on Veridian Four was saved because the ship was sacrificed. Every captain wishes such an end for his vessel."

O'Brien nodded. "That's why I became an engineer. I'd rather build 'em than wreck 'em. How's the rest of the crew taking it?"

"We are Starfleet officers," Worf said. "We take things."

Rewarding him with a laugh of mutuality, O'Brien didn't ask again. He either understood what Worf meant or understood that the Klingon didn't want to be the courier of other people's feelings, especially about such a thing as the loss of their vessel.

It felt good to talk to O'Brien, to walk beside him again even in the bout of silence that came now as they both imagined their crewmates and the ship on which they had served together. He wondered if O'Brien felt guilty for having transferred off the ship to this distant spiral in the dark. Probably not. O'Brien had left the *Enterprise* in excellent condition and come here to a place where an innovative engineer was desperately needed. And, Worf knew, the chance to convert a Cardassian station to Starfleet equipment. The textbooks went out the nearest portal. A hungry task, a lengthy purpose with a horizon.

They passed a huddle of Ferengi and deliberately kept moving. Worf noticed that O'Brien maneuvered between him and the Ferengi, attempting a buffer zone—as if that would stop anything that insisted upon happening. Ferengi didn't like Klingons, but didn't usually try anything physical.

One of them, intimidated enough to stay behind in the crowd but bold enough to speak up, said, "Just what this station needs. Another Klingon."

Worf glanced at O'Brien. They kept walking. In his life among humans, striving as his adoptive parents encouraged to remain as Klingon as possible, Worf had heard the word *Klingon* used as everything from compliment to epithet. No use of it bothered him anymore. He listened only to tone, inflection, and peered into the eyes of anyone who said it, for there was the true opinion.

"That was Quark, wasn't it?" he rumbled quietly.

"You'll have to forgive him," O'Brien said. "The presence of the Klingon task force in his bar's been costing him."

"I understand." What he really meant was that he didn't care, but no point starting off on that note.

He could tell from O'Brien's amused glance that his attitude hadn't gone missed.

"We'll square away your gear," the engineer said. "Then you can report in."

"With Major Kira? Or Commander Sisko."

"Oh—you haven't heard? It's *Captain* Sisko now."

"Is it . . . that will be easier to say."

"Easier to 'say'?"

"There is something about addressing myself to a captain which comes naturally to me."

O'Brien smiled. "I can relate to that. Starship duty'll do that to a person. I don't envy you. I know why Sisko asked Starfleet Command to find you."

"To deal with other Klingons."

"Right. Some of the force has moved off, but there are still a bundle of 'em here. And these Klingons, they've been in space a long time. They're the hardened ones, left over after all the weaker ones have been killed or couldn't take the pressure of deep space. You're here to deal with them."

"Do not worry, Chief," Worf offered. "They will relate to *me.*"

O'Brien grinned again.

"Tell me, Chief," Worf asked, "why does Captain Sisko think these Klingons need to be dealt with?"

"I don't know it it's for me to say. I'm sure he'll tell you his concerns. . . ."

"Yes, but I would like your opinion."

"Don't know if I have one. There's just been a strange, well, sort of quietly hostile air around here. The Klingons haven't even been acting like—you'll pardon this, but . . . Klingons."

"Yes. I saw all the ships. I am certain something is under way. After all, stealth is not the Klingons' greatest talent."

"No. Say, if you do have to rough it up any, you can do us a favor. You can start with a joker named Drex. He took a poke at Garak."

"Your Cardassian tailor?"

"Well, he's a tailor at the moment. With Garak, we can never tell. But he's living here, he's one of us, and we don't take kindly to having our neighbors pounded."

"How do you know he did not provoke the attack?"

"Because, as I hear it, he was with Odo at the time, and Odo wouldn't have allowed him to 'provoke' anybody. Whatever was said, the Klingons took it harder than they should've. They took Garak four to one."

"Four to one is dishonorable," Worf told him. "Unless the one is me."

"Lieutenant Commander Worf reporting for duty."

The stars were a passive, challenging backdrop out the viewing portals of the commander's—the captain's—office. Worf covered the space between the door and the desk in two strides.

Before him, Captain Sisko swung around from watching those stars. "It's good to have you aboard, Commander."

"Thank you, sir." Worf didn't look Sisko in the face, but kept his shoulders straight, his arms at his sides, and his chin up. As a captain, Sisko deserved to see, once in a while, someone standing at attention.

Sisko's expression betrayed his enjoyment of the small offering. "At ease, Mr. Worf. I was sorry to hear about the *Enterprise*. She was a good ship."

"Yes, sir," Worf responded clinically. A good ship—there was no better way to say in three words what a ship like the *Enterprise* really was, or the *Enterprise* that had come before her, the heritage of slam and sacrifice, of first-through-the-door danger that she represented.

That ship had been a warrior. Her death was appropriate.

"I understand you've been on leave," Sisko said, and it was obvious he was changing the subject on purpose.

Relieved that he was not expected to discuss the ship, Worf blandly acknowledged, "Yes, I have been visiting the Klingon monastery on Boreth. I found my discussions with the clerics there most enlightening."

"I hope you'll forgive us for pulling you away from your studies. I doubt this assignment will last very long."

"My leave was almost over."

"Any idea where you'll be stationed next?" Sisko asked him.

So he had picked up on Worf's hint that he wasn't going back to Boreth, but didn't want to outrightly *say* that he didn't want to go back. Again Worf was relieved, but kept it out of his face.

Yet he knew he wasn't fooling Sisko.

Struck with a flash of candidness, he said, "I am considering resigning my commission."

"Really?" Sisko's face changed for the first time. "Do you mind if I ask why?"

"I have spent most of my life among humans," Worf found himself saying. Perhaps the time on Boreth had made him less guarded, for he spoke openly to a man whom he hardly knew. "It has not always been easy for me. And since the destruction of the *Enterprise,* it has become even more difficult. I am no longer sure I belong in this uniform."

Sisko absorbed the words, the concept, the struggle that not all, but many Starfleet officers faced at one time or another in their lives—to keep putting on the uniform today, tomorrow, the next day. He seemed to comprehend professionally, but also personally.

He paced from one end of his desk to the other. "Mr. Worf, if I said we didn't need you, I'd be lying. But if you don't want to take this assignment . . . I'd understand."

"Thank you, sir," Worf said quickly. "But until I make my decision, I intend to do my duty."

"I'm glad to hear that. I assume you've read my situation report."

Worf nodded, but didn't mention that O'Brien had given him the nonofficial take on what was happening and that he thought the picture was ugly, but clear.

Sisko didn't prod. "I can't help feeling that General Martok hasn't told me the whole truth about the

Klingon task force. There are too many unanswered questions."

"Then I will attempt to find you the answers."

Worf made the simple offering because he knew it was hoped for, if not expected. Captain Sisko had requested Worf's assistance, but hadn't been able to specify, officially, any more than a need for a presence with Starfleet authority that the Klingons would instinctively respect, or at least to which they would pay attention.

"Good," Sisko said, hinting at his relief that Worf understood and wasn't insulted. "If you need any help, let me know."

"Yes, sir."

Worf turned to exit. He needed no explanations of what to do first. That would be his to decide. By not specifying, by not assigning him escort, by not asking questions, Sisko was giving him free hand to act as he wished.

"Commander," Sisko said just before Worf made it to the door. "I just wanted to say . . . I thought about resigning from Starfleet once too. But I know now, if I had, I would've regretted it." He paused, searched for thoughts, then added, "I guess what I'm saying is . . . don't make any hasty decisions."

The words seemed shallow, awkward from one officer to another, but there was substance beneath them. Sisko was evidently hoping Worf would assume that, would comprehend the inner torture signaled by what he was saying. The details wouldn't help.

The fact that another officer had gone through this—did.

"Thank you, sir," Worf said. "I will keep that in mind."

Garak puttered in his tailor shop. When there was little work, puttering became his art. An annoyance, but it kept up appearances. As many times before, he found himself thinking of his earliest years, stitching carpet samples and making fabric patterns for his uncle's furniture factory. Who would have known that such mundane childhood drudgery would come in so handy? If he were not a tailor, what excuse could he have to linger on *Deep Space Nine,* the nearest Federation outpost to Cardassian space?

He could keep a tavern, but Quark already did that here. He could open some other kind of shop, but there already were dozens of misplaced beings running cubicles here, trying to sell things they appropriated from various sources. In fact, shops came and went here constantly. The average length of stay for a business was only one or two months. He needed longer than that.

So, he not only opened a shop, but provided a service. Those who did not buy clothing at least occasionally ripped clothing. Beings appeared here who needed special fittings. After all, a creature with the head of a fish and the body of a spiny tree could hardly buy a shirt off the rack.

And now and then—not frequently, but significantly—he had a chance to use his position here to do a small favor for *Deep Space Nine,* forsaken though it was.

He grinned as he thought of Drex. The big bully

would take the information he had "wrenched" from Garak and give it to his leader. He would puff up with pride that he had taken the details and he would probably be congratulated. Then, when the truth came out—and it would, in time—Drex would be seen as the pawn of a Cardassian spy and would be humiliated.

Grinning again, Garak wondered what the Klingons would do to Drex. He wondered if there weren't some way he could help do it. Skin peeling or tongue pinning . . .

He glanced up as one browsing customer left and another strode in, and his hand began to shake.

A Klingon. Big one. Unfamiliar.

This one was standing behind the high rack of ceremonial robes, glancing around at the merchandise, but didn't seem particularly interested in any item.

Despite the fact that he had purposely orchestrated the events that left his back sore and his legs aching, Garak hesitated to approach another of the evolutionarily deprived.

Did they want more from him? Worse—had they discovered that the information he provided was bogus and out of date?

Perforce he shook off his fright enough to function. He had to appear casual. Maybe they weren't sure yet and were watching him for suspicious behavior.

Of course, there was another, slightly bizarre, possibility. This one could be shopping.

He moved forward, staying on the opposite side of the rack of robes.

"May I help you, sir?"

The Klingon looked up. "You are Garak."

It wasn't a question.

"I'm glad to hear my reputation is spreading. Is there some garment I can enlarge for you?"

"No, thank you." The Klingon came around the ceremonial robes in two strides—

A Starfleet uniform! An officer?

"I am Lieutenant Commander Worf, Starfleet Security. I'm here to investigate the assault upon you by Klingon nationals visiting this station."

"But . . . isn't station security Constable Odo's venue, Lieutenant Commander? I've already spoken to Captain Sisko, and I assumed—"

"This is not station security. This is *Starfleet* security. I've come to monitor the actions of Klingons, specifically, and you were attacked by Klingons—"

"Specifically." Garak nodded. "They came in, four of them, I offered them my tailoring services, and they gave me a most improper thrashing. That's all I know. Perhaps I can offer you a quick cup of strained *gagh?*"

"No, thank you."

"I didn't think so."

"I will have coffee."

"You will?"

"Yes. Cream and sugar."

"I'll . . . get it."

Garak meandered through the displayed clothing, belts, shoes, and jewelry to the shop replicator. If he could get this one angry, the subject would change and then the lieutenant commander would lose his chain of thought and ultimately leave. Garak made a bet that the uniform prevented the big Klingon from lashing out, but it was a thin bet and he was careful to stay out of arm's swipe.

"You don't want any small animals in the coffee . . . mice, insects?" he called back.

The lieutenant commander scowled at him, but simply said, "No, thank you."

Strange, very strange. Didn't this one know a proper insult when he heard one?

"Very well," Garak said, and spoke to the replicator's sensor track. "Coffee, cream and sugar, no mice. Well, lieutenant commander, I reported the assault and the doctor glued me back together, and I'm cautiously getting along with my life, if it can properly be called that. If you wish to know what happened, you can—"

"I have already read the report. I am interested in what is missing from the report."

Such a voice. Garak shuddered. "And what is it you think is missing?"

"What they wanted from you."

"From me? I can't imagine. I assumed they just didn't care for Cardassians. Some people are like that, you know. The crude among us . . . Have you seen these gem-studded mirrors?"

The lieutenant commander ignored his own face reflected in the mirror Garak held up just as he said "crude," and simply said, "I do not believe that."

"You don't . . ."

"No. And I find your situation on the station to be very odd. You are an outcast, apparently not by choice. What would you do in order to get back into favor with the Cardassians who are keeping you out?"

Taken aback, Garak stared at him briefly. Then he mustered a mental shield and said, "I opened my door to Klingons—whatever *else* could be expected of a person?"

He leaned away a little more, then reached out—way out—to hand the coffee over.

The lieutenant commander's black eyes flared and Garak waited for the wind tunnel of angry roaring.

"Mr. Garak," the calm voice said instead—calm?—"I am attempting to narrow down the reasons an organized team of Klingons would target you, an exiled civilian, out of a station rife with military officials. I conclude that there was some information they wanted from you. And I want to know whether or not you gave it to them. I have made myself clear. Please do the same."

He wasn't getting mad. Why wasn't he getting mad?

Garak stared into his face, and into the plain fact that he might have misjudged. Evidence stood before him that not all Klingons were so predictable. Here was one who wasn't acting at all like a Klingon. What if it had been *this* Klingon who had come after him for information about *Deep Space Nine?*

"What is it worth to you," the lieutenant commander persisted, "to get back with your own people?"

Lowering his arms to his sides in a kind of giving-up motion, Garak said, "I haven't tallied that price tag quite yet, Lieutenant Commander."

"You are hiding something. Drex and his troops obviously did not assault you frivolously. You know something, yet you fail to help us understand what the Klingon Empire is planning. Captain Sisko and his crew have protected you, let you remain here despite the possibility of repercussions from whoever over-powered you on Cardassia, yet you will not cooperate. I do not know you, yet already I do not respect you, Mr. Garak. Silence is also a betrayal."

This soldier was not behaving at all like a Klingon. In spite of his contempt, there was no blustering or fang-showing. Garak had succeeded in making him angry, but not as planned. The Klingon was treating Garak like something to be scraped off a boot—and Garak was actually disturbed.

He tried to muster his sly smile, but failed. How odd and how stimulating to be beaten by a Klingon, without so much as a slap.

"All right," he said finally, and decided that this lieutenant commander deserved a reward for his win. "It's true, they wanted information. But I did nothing—*nothing*, Lieutenant Commander—to harm Captain Sisko or this station. You're right that I don't like being an outcast and I don't intend to remain an outcast. But if I were willing to do 'any-thing' to get back in, you may believe I would be back in already. I intend to go back, but on my own terms. What price will I pay? A high one, to be sure, but not *any* price. I don't know what put you in this uniform instead of Klingon body armor, but somehow I think you know what I'm talking about. No one should be willing to pay *anything* for anything. Do you under-stand? I think so. Now, perhaps we can dispense with this ugly business and find you a nice garment with historical significance. This is called a Nehru jacket . . . it goes very well with the Hessian boots."

* * *

"Let me guess! Klingon bloodwine."

"Prune juice, chilled."

Worf made his order, then glared down, down, down at the guileful Ferengi barkeeper's wide eyes and elephantine ears without flinching.

Before him, Quark forced himself not to blink. "Prune juice? . . . If you say so . . ."

When the bartender went to dicker with the replicator, Worf leaned on the bar and slowly surveyed his new environment. The patrons milled about in undeniable tension. In the darker corners were Klingons, as aware of him as he was of them. They knew he wasn't one of their fleet, for he wore his Starfleet uniform with his Klingon bandoleer over one shoulder. He deliberately leaned into one of the bands of light threading through the dark bar. He was here to be seen.

"Commander!"

Worf turned. Miles O'Brien was motioning to him from where he stood with someone else, a lightly built young man with a narrow face and large eyes, wearing a medical uniform.

Taking the prune juice wordlessly provided by Quark, Worf decided he could surveil the premises from the table as well as the bar. Better, perhaps.

"Dr. Julian Bashir," O'Brien said, gesturing to the medic. "Lieutenant Commander Worf."

The doctor held up a dart. "Care for a game of darts?"

"I do not play games." Worf tried to sound apologetic, but it didn't come out right. He never could get that conciliatory tone just right.

"It's like poker," O'Brien quipped, "but with pointy tips."

Worf realized he might have insulted them, but he was aware of the eyes of other Klingons in the bar. This wasn't the right image if he was going to have the respect of those strangers.

"All right," O'Brien attempted again, "think of it as target practice."

Bashir's voice was mellow. "The object is to throw the dart and hit the board over there."

"Aim for the red dot in the middle," O'Brien added.

Realizing that O'Brien was getting a chuckle out of Bashir's unfamiliarity with Worf, that the doctor didn't realize Worf had been raised by humans and perfectly well knew what darts were, Worf cast the engineer a scolding glower. Now wasn't the time to explain his background to the doctor. Those Klingons could overhear.

He took the dart, held it like a throwing dagger, and flung it at the board, using his arm all the way up to the shoulder. The dart didn't hit the bull's-eye, but it did bury itself two inches into the board. Splinters danced to the floor.

He stood straight. His moment of possible embarrassment might have turned in his favor. The Klingons were still watching.

With a nod at the dartboard, then at O'Brien and Bashir, he turned wordlessly from the game, still holding his glass of prune juice.

As he turned away, the doctor's smooth voice murmured, "I think the patient did not survive."

Worf hoped he hadn't insulted the doctor, but impressions were everything, and not for Bashir. He stopped short as two women descended a stairway that had until now been hidden by the architecture of this place. They were dressed in fairy-tale princess gowns, with huge pointed hats and long veils.

"I can't believe you did that," the dark-haired one said, and as she descended Worf could see the spotted trail of skin mottling around her hairline and down her neck that marked her as a Trill.

"He didn't leave me any choice," the other girl said in a fierce tone that didn't match the daintiness of her attire.

Bashir looked up at them. "What did she do?"

The Trill smiled—a stunning change. "She knocked out Lancelot!"

The other woman unapologetically claimed, "He kissed me!"

"He's supposed to kiss you."

"But I was playing a married woman!"

So these people had a holodeck, and these women were in a holonovel of some sort. Classical Earth literature. Knights. Damsels. The Trill fit the part, but the other one was no damsel.

The two paused as they saw Worf, and the red-haired woman quickly scanned his Starfleet uniform and Klingon bandoleer, and her expression changed.

"Lieutenant Commander Worf," the doctor introduced, "this is Lieutenant Commander Jadzia Dax and Major Kira Nerys, our first officer."

Worf nodded to Major Nerys. No—he saw now that she was Bajoran. Major Kira, then.

"Nice hat," he said.

The major quickly pulled the hat off her head, revealing very short hair. "I don't always dress like this. We were in the holosuites."

"So I gathered." He turned to the other woman. "You used to be Curzon Dax."

"That's right," the elegant commander said, but unlike the major she was not defensive at all. "And I don't usually dress this way either."

"Curzon's name is an honored one among my people," Worf offered.

Dax smiled mischievously and spoke to him in clear Klingon: *"Yes, but I'm a lot better-looking than he was."*

Struck with unease at this Dax's lack of respect for the previous host of the consciousness she carried, Worf muttered, "I suppose so. Excuse me."

Fate had provided him with a reason to escape— the Klingon called Drex and two of his companions had just lumbered into the bar. O'Brien had pointed him out to Worf when they passed him on the way to Worf's quarters, but that hadn't been a good time for a confrontation.

This was.

As he moved away from the women and O'Brien and Bashir, he heard Kira murmur, "What did you say to him?"

Dax didn't lower her voice. "It loses something in the translation."

"This bloodwine is cold!" Drex was shouting at a Ferengi waiter. "Get me another!"

Quark swung by and leaned toward the waiter to tell him, "Do as he says." Then he muttered, "But charge him double."

Glancing at the Ferengi, Worf wondered whether the fast dealer intended to live out the day, but Drex evidently hadn't heard him.

Worf stepped forward. "You are Drex, son of Martok."

The other Klingon surveyed him with disapproval. "That's right."

"I am Worf, son of Mogh."

Without further announcement, he wound up and slammed Drex full in the face, knocking him hard against the bar with a clatter of glassware. Stunned, Drex clawed for his dagger, but Worf lathered a combination of fists across Drex's bleeding face. The other Klingon slid along the bar and slumped to the deck, unconscious.

Worf spun around instantly, knowing what was coming toward him—all the other Klingons in the bar. But he also saw in their faces that they were shocked, unsure how to react, and they knew what he had just done.

They backed away from his harsh glare. When they stepped back and he felt fairly assured of a buffer zone, he bent over and pulled Drex's dagger out, placed it in his own belt, and went out of the bar with measured strides.

He had drawn the line.

CHAPTER
10

"ENTER."

It was happening, very quickly. Something about the ring of his door chime annoyed him. Klingon predictability. The rule of mass habit.

He frowned at the personal items he had just laid out from his duffel bag. His *bat'leth* lay on the blanket, its curved form and razor-edged tines seeming incongruous there beside his Fleet-issue phaser, his items of off-duty clothing, and a picture of his son, Alexander.

The door chime saved him from gazing too long at the picture, from doubting his decision to leave Alexander on Earth after the destruction of their only mutual home, the ship.

The massive Klingon who came in the door of his quarters was boiling with anger.

"I have come for my son's *d'k tahg*. Give it to me or I will take it from you!"

Another crick of disappointment. Predictability had done its job. This was Martok, reacting exactly in line with Worf's deliberate actions in the bar. Do this, and he will do that.

To Martok's clear startlement, Worf simply handed him the dagger.

"Now that you are here," he told the general, "I have no further need of it."

Martok stared at the dagger, stunned. This was worse to him than having to fight for it.

"You robbed my son of his honor," he rumbled, "just to get my attention?"

His voice actually squeaked at the end.

Worf blandly said, "You cannot take away what someone does not have."

Gravely offended, Martok lowered his chin and stared out from under his brow ridge. "Are you saying my son is without honor?"

"I am saying your son is a coward and a liar."

"And what of his father?"

"That remains to be seen?"

Thoroughly baffled, Martok hesitated, began to speak, paused again, then began again. "Tell me . . . what have I done to earn your disrespect?"

"The misdeeds your troops have committed speak for themselves," Worf told him. "Assaulting a Cardassian citizen, detaining and searching ships in neutral space without warning or provocation, and you—executing one of your own commanding officers because he refused to fire on a Federation ship."

Martok hurled, "Whatever we have done is in the best interest of the Alpha Quadrant!"

"You must take me for a fool to make your lies so transparent."

Worf stood him down and let the strong statement fester, but Martok saw what Worf was trying to do and kept control of himself.

"I do not wish to quarrel with you," the general said.

"Nor I with you," Worf allowed. "Your house is an honored one, with a proud tradition. But I need to know why you are here."

"I am here under the authority of Gowron himself. I am carrying out his orders. That should be all the explanation a Klingon warrior needs."

Martok was emphatic, but there was a tinge of overstatement in his tone, as if he were desperately trying to agree with himself and hoping Worf would buy the performance.

"You forget," Worf said, "I am not just a Klingon warrior. I am a Starfleet officer. And Starfleet deserves an explanation."

"They will get one soon enough," Martok evaded. "But until then, know this—my mission will determine the fate of the Klingon Empire. Interfere, and you risk destroying us all!"

PART
TWO

PART

TWO

CHAPTER
11

THEY WHO HAVE fierce enemies invent fierce legends.

One of those came at Worf through an opal haze, an ogre out of the cruelest story of defeat, and the monster's noise was a terrible noise.

Blow upon blow rang on Worf's bones, his weapon flashing to petty avail, his body aching and his grace of form completely botched.

The monster's face was compounded in its ugliness by the hologram computer's twisted idea of the bizarre, angles of olive light and moldings of flesh that only a machine could invent. Tell a computer to picture a real animal and it would do a prime job. Tell it to conjure a legend, and it went insane.

He fought and fought, and no matter how he panted or stumbled, the computer refused to turn off. He had it set on its maximum, only to find that this computer, unlike the tame beasts on the *Enterprise,* had been programmed to give a "customer" what he actually said he wanted. The starship had known better.

Quark did not.

As so with roar after spit after howl of the ogre's raw throat and poison breath, Worf was being beaten back.

"You shouldn't drop your left arm like that."

The voice came out of the quartz-gray fog, and there in the dripping jungle stood the outline of that woman who used to be Curzon Dax, standing against the now-closing exit from the holosuite.

Momentarily distracted, Worf heard the swish of the ogre's attack, and only narrowly skated out of the way.

"I do not recall," he panted, "asking for your advice."

"Just trying to help."

Inspired now that he had an audience—and he could not tell how many personalities were watching him at the moment—Worf launched into a torrent of dodges and hits, basting the monster in the face, throttling it when its shoulder dipped, and finally knocking its bleeding legs out from under it. The creature staggered, crumpled, and finally dematerialized.

"So," this Dax said, "how'd you like the program?"

"I found it adequate," Worf lied, hiding his heavy breathing as much as he could. "Though I was surprised to find a Klingon exercise program in this holosuite."

"It's mine," she told him with a touch of swagger as she approached.

"You mean Curzon's."

"No. I mean mine. Computer, *bat'leth.*"

Worf's weapon was stuck in the ground a few feet to his side. Now another *bat'leth* appeared beside it, replicated to solidity by the fabulous technology around them.

"I thought you might be tired of fighting programs," Dax said.

Straightening with some effort, Worf declined. "It would not be a fair match."

She smiled. "I'll go easy on you."

Woman, man, young, old. Impossible to tell. What she knew, what she could do, what she could not.

It was not for Worf to measure.

"Very well," he decided. "Defend yourself."

He took up his own *bat'leth* and adjusted the balance in his hands. It was a good thing, this weapon. A good sensation, putting a strong weapon forward. He knew his was the superior strength, heavy of body and possessing raw power, and that would serve, but he wasn't so foolish that he didn't note her lightness of body and therefore superior speed and agility. In his years aboard the starship he had seen many adversaries in many forms and had discovered, as he had tried to tell Lourn, that power of meat and fury had found its blunt limit in advancement of technology, experience, and intelligence, which could equalize anything and anyone.

Proof of that maneuvered before him now. She was a girl, half his weight, half his age, a feather-light humanoid without a male's upper-body strength, and yet she hid a deadly secret. The experience of—how many lifetimes? Eight? Ten? Worf knew he would never have that.

And Dax was no fool. She knew that Curzon had made many enemies, as had the personalities before him. She probably had her own share. She had to be ready for that. Most people only dealt with the enemies of a few decades. She had to be ready for the enemies of centuries.

The two of them began to fence. He did as best he knew, plunged at her with considered balance, and not surprisingly she parried out of his way and landed a blow on his shoulder. If they had been out to kill each other, she would've taken his head off from the back with that blow.

His shoulder went numb down to the elbow and though he was holding the curved *bat'leth* in two hands, only one was any good. As the feeling trickled back into his hand he twisted to face her.

"I see you have not forgotten all that Curzon knew about the *bat'leth.*"

She grinned as she fielded his swipes and thrusts. "I've even learned a few tricks of my own."

She fell to the defensive for one instant, enough to make him step to one side and put all his balance on one leg. Then the offensive was hers, and her combination put Worf staggering. She almost scored another hit.

"I hope you're not holding back because I'm a woman," she said. "If it makes things easier, think of me as a man. I *have* been one several times."

In answer, not because he was holding back against

a woman, but because the woman assumed he was, Worf blew into a whirlwind of strikes, driving her back. Finally he swept her legs from beneath her, and she struck the ground hard on her back.

Heaving into the fabricated mist, Worf breathed, "You're right. That was easier."

With a wince and a shuffle of her heels on the gravel, she looked up at him and smiled. "Feel better?"

He scowled down, brows drawn. What did she mean? Every one of her sentences had something underneath.

"I take it," she went on, "your conversation with General Martok didn't go all that well."

Extending her hand, she reverted to her more obvious form—feminine—and waited until he got the message and drew her to her feet.

"He was not forthcoming," Worf said. "And he is not the only one. I tried contacting Gowron, Emperor Kahless, even my own brother who sits on the High Council. No one will speak to me."

As he said all that, he realized something about the litany of silences. At first he had thought all these people were avoiding him because of his Starfleet connections, but suddenly he realized that couldn't be all. His brother, at least, would speak to him.

This ringing silence—was it not in its own way an answer? That all these highly placed Klingons felt unable to speak . . . there was something in that.

"Maybe you're going about this the wrong way," Dax said to him.

She seemed to be reading his expression and the jingle of awareness that had come to his eyes.

"With so many Klingons around, there must be someone who owes your family a favor."

"And the blood was ankle deep . . .
And the River Skral ran crimson red
On the day above all days
When Kahless slew evil Molor dead!"

"Hah!"

Bloodwine, song, and the tradition of recalling the victorious past—and a butting of skulls, then laughter.

The laughter was to hide the headache.

With the room spinning around him, Worf reeled back and laughed very hard indeed. Beside him, his Klingon father's warrior-companion Huraga was drunk to staggering.

That was why they were both sitting down.

"Your father and I," the old Klingon slurred, "used to sing that song when you were just a small boy. Did I ever tell you how your father saved my family's honor during our blood feud with the House of Duras?"

"Many times," Worf uttered, pretending to be more drunk than he was. Well, pretending some. "Including twice this evening."

"It is a good story."

"You tell it well."

"Your father was a great warrior. My family owes him everything we have. I wish there was some way I could repay him."

Every now and then, an opportunity dropped into a person's hand which was so obvious and so easy that only the dead would fail to notice. Worf leaned closer to the old man.

"There is," he said. "Tell me why the task force is here. The real reason . . . not the one Martok has given the Federation."

Huraga regarded him with age-glazed eyes. "The real reason? I suppose you have a right to know. You are a Klingon warrior and it would be wrong to keep you away from battle. And it is going to be a *glorious* battle. . . ."

The old man was dreaming old dreams, Worf could tell, yet his words were in the present well enough. He was anticipating what would come and didn't want Worf to miss it. He assumed that Worf, like he himself, lived for battle and hungered for it, found his only identity there, and his only chance for honorable death. Perhaps Huraga hoped to fight again, long enough to die with a weapon in his hand. Some Klingons would start feuds just to die that way. Peace was hard on a warrior.

He looked at Huraga. Could the old man see his Klingon blood diluting?

Huraga was smiling at him. He would talk in his own time, draw the truth out until it tantalized.

"There are races in the galaxy, Worf," the old Klingon began, very slowly, speaking past the effects of the bloodwine, "who are made to conflict with each other. It is their nature. *Our* nature."

Worf nodded. "Yes, others have told me this."

He realized with a jump of his stomach that he may have made a mistake, that he should've stayed quiet. The old man was talking. Let it flow.

But Huraga inhaled deeply and let out a smelly

heave. "And so are the Cardassians. Built and bred to battle. Big. Mean. Angry. Possessive. Strong. And they know it."

With each word Worf offered only a nod.

"They have revolted on their world," Huraga went on. "Kicked out the rulers who have retreated from so many conquests."

"An uprising?" Worf coughed. "On Cardassia Prime?"

"I would rise up!" Huraga raised his hand and shook it in the air. "I would shake out the weaklings who retreat in the face of challenge!"

"Yes, I know you would—"

"I would pull the skulls from the necks of cowards who step back when the sword is at their necks! I would!"

"I believe you, Huraga."

"Fight! Fight! Kick! Bite!" The old man rattled the ceiling with his shout, then elbowed back another swig of the bloodwine while the echo fell. "Ahhhh!" he gulped out. He didn't look at Worf, but stared into the low light. "But even an uprising will not save them . . . they know not their enemy."

Worf leaned toward him. "What do you mean?"

"Their enemy . . . is the Dominion. Yes—I see the shock in your face. I was shocked too, but that is the truth. I spoke to Gowron himself and he told me the overthrow was puppeted by those slimy interferers from the Gamma Quadrant. They have seeped through and they are here now."

"But how do you know this?" Worf prodded. "Have you seen a changeling? Has Gowron seen them?"

The old man's eyes flared. "They cannot be seen.

They can melt into the wall. But they are here. You know . . . it is too bad."

Before Worf's eyes, Huraga sighed as if he weren't looking forward to what was coming as much as he had pretended.

"Too bad . . ." he said again.

"What do you mean?" Worf asked.

"Oh . . . only the cloud of age, Worf." He took another swig of the wine. "You know, we've been at peace a long time. These young warriors, they don't know what war really is. I'm old. I've seen it. I got a chance to live out my life in a time when we all pretended we did not wish to live it out. But we did, Worf. Anyone wants to live. You know," he said, looking up suddenly, "there's a problem with dying with honor. You have to die to do it."

He sagged back, holding the neck of the wine bottle with one hand and clasping Worf's arm with the other.

Abruptly he laughed. "Worf! I know what to do! They should send all us old soldiers to go and die! We're ready!" He rolled back with laughter. "An army of the old, sick, and diseased! And don't forget the ugly women! We can do without them too! Hah! Hah-hah!"

The image of such an army marched across the old man's face and flushed him with delight. Soon he was gasping, and the laughter faded away.

Worf felt uncomfortable. He said nothing. There was nothing more to say.

Huraga sighed again, and seemed less drunk than he had a moment ago.

"So war comes," the old Klingon said. "And we are

called upon to squash the changelings before their poison flows into the blood of our quadrant. The Cardassians have fallen to revolution. That wasn't easy. The Obsidian Order was ruthless. It was purposeful and dangerous. Why are they suddenly kicked out? There has been another power involved, greater than the Cardassian populace. That is the only answer. The Dominion is here, Worf . . . you and all the other young warriors will be Klingon against them . . . and you must kill them all."

CHAPTER
12

THE ENEMY MATERIALIZED beside him. So smooth and so silent was the enemy's approach that the warrior had not seen, smelled, or heard him coming.

Stealth. It would be the death of Alpha Quadrant.

And no one could master stealth like a changeling.

"It all seems simpler from up here, doesn't it?" the changeling said.

Worf inched a little down the railing on the upper walkways as he stood above the Promenade and watched the varied denizens of *Deep Space Nine* mill about below, including Klingons.

Beside him, Constable Odo gazed down.

Hating the efficiency with which Odo had come up on him from behind, Worf bluntly said, "If you are looking to start a conversation, look somewhere else. I prefer to be left alone."

"Maybe," the shapeshifter said, his plasticlike face expressionless. "But you can't stay up here forever. Sooner or later you're going to have to talk to Captain Sisko. Whatever you've found out about the Klingons, he should be the first to know."

Anger pierced Worf's layer of defensive privacy. "You have been spying on me."

Odo wasn't intimidated. "As chief of security, it's my duty to observe the inhabitants of this station. Since your arrival, you've transmitted an average of five messages a day to the Klingon Homeworld . . . none of which have gotten a response."

Feeling all this show on his face, Worf hardened his own expression, but knew he had failed to bury the facts. Odo was reading him like a computer screen.

"Then last night," the shapeshifter went on, "you met with a Klingon officer in your quarters. And since then you haven't sent a single message. In fact, you've done nothing to further your investigation of the Klingon task force."

"None of which is your business," Worf attempted, shifting his posture.

"The security of this station *is* my business. And your behavior leads me to conclude that either you've given up your investigation, in which case it's my duty to take over . . . or you've found something. Something so disturbing that you're hesitant to inform Captain Sisko."

"I am not interested in your conclusions."

Worf tried and failed to keep control of his tone. The security chief's deductions were flawless, and there would be no keeping secret the fact that he knew the secret. Odo would go to Sisko if Worf did not, but was giving Worf the chance to take the first step as he had been assigned to do, to fulfill his responsibility as an officer of Starfleet first, and set his genetic identity second.

Feeling his defense crumble under the weight of his terrible knowledge and Odo's perceptiveness, Worf swung around and tried to stride away. He had to go away, or let slip his innate racial propensities, which came so naturally and which were so reprehensible.

"Commander," the shapeshifter called, and Worf turned back. "I just wanted to say that I understand what you're going through. I've also had to choose between my duty and loyalty to my people."

Dismissively Worf said, "I have read your Starfleet security file."

"Frankly, Mr. Worf, I don't care which choice you make. But you owe it to Captain Sisko to let him know which side you're on," the constable finished flatly, "before it's too late. Enjoy the view."

"Mr. Worf . . ."

Ben Sisko gestured the Klingon into his office after releasing the officers who had been giving him a debriefing on outer-hull integrity of the station. The hull had made it twenty-odd years. An hour or two wouldn't change much.

So they went out and the Klingon came in, incongruous as ever with his Starfleet livery and that silver bandoleer of a warrior.

Worf didn't want to be here. That was clear in his bearing.

Circling around him to the other side of the desk, in a way of making this official, Sisko studied Worf and gave him time to get used to the conversation that was coming, to find words for whatever he had to say. The trouble of it showed in Worf's face. He wasn't anxious to speak. His face was stone.

The answers, it seemed, were an arm's length away, if he didn't chase them off by pushing.

But if Worf's didn't speak up pretty damned soon, they were both going to strangle from the suspense.

"Captain . . ." The Klingon was forcing himself.

For a flash Sisko worried that perhaps the answers weren't here after all and Worf was coming to report an utter failure.

No, that wasn't it.

"Yes, Commander?" he nudged patiently.

"The news . . . is not good."

Sisko offered a half nod. "I stopped expecting good news when the task force showed up under cloak, Commander. We're Starfleet officers. We take bad news well enough. Do you have a report for me?"

Worf's rugged face flushed plum-brown. Was that embarrassment? Was it shame?

"Go ahead, Commander," Sisko encouraged. "Whatever you found out, it's not your fault."

"No," Worf said, suddenly meeting his eyes for the first time, "but it is the doings of my people . . . other Klingons. All the Klingons. All . . . but me."

Something snapped. Sisko felt his charity fall away and with it went his patience. "That's racist claptrap and you know it or you wouldn't be in that uniform. Now give me my report."

Worf snapped back to attention and seemed even more embarrassed, perhaps legitimately this time.

"Sir . . . I regret to inform you of impending invasion by the Klingons."

"Invasion on us, here?"

"No, sir. By the Klingon Empire . . . on Cardassia."

Sisko came out from behind his desk. "Cardassia? Why would the Klingons want to invade Cardassia!"

Uneasily Worf gathered his thoughts and forced them into words. "According to my source, there's been an uprising on the Cardassian homeworld. The Central Command has been overthrown and power has been transferred to civilian authorities."

"Even if your source is correct, what does that have to do with the Klingons?"

Worf's eyes narrowed and the tight lids flinched as if he were in pain somewhere on that massive body.

"Gowron and the High Council," he struggled on, "believe that the coup was engineered by the Dominion."

As if he'd been slapped, Sisko was driven to ask, "Do they have any proof?"

"None that I know of." The admittance of this, of the plain nature of his information as hearsay, made Worf flush again. "But they are convinced that civilians could not have overthrown the Central Command without help."

"So by attacking Cardassia, they think they're protecting the Alpha Quadrant from the Dominion."

"So they believe."

The logic was faulty, full of holes, details sketchy and questionable. Worf didn't appear any more comfortable with giving this report than was Sisko in hearing it. Answers which made no more sense than the questions were uncomforting.

Sisko glared at him, then keyed his comm. "Sisko to Dax. Contact General Martok. Tell him I need to meet with him immediately."

"Yes, sir."

"Mr. Worf, I know this hasn't been an easy assignment for you," Sisko began, without knowing what he would say next. Was it appropriate to apologize for requiring an officer to do a duty to which he was best suited, for whatever reason, at whatever cost? No.

"No," Worf said, as if echoing Sisko's very thoughts. He seemed to relax a little. "But I knew this day would come. Ever since I joined Starfleet, I knew I might be forced to choose between the Federation and the Klingon Empire."

Sisko straightened. "Maybe you don't have to make that decision just yet. I don't think there's any need for you to be here when I meet with Martok."

Handed a sudden choice, Worf stared at Sisko and evidently was now torn in a third direction. He had just been given a way out, a chance to remain anonymous in the discovery of this disturbing news, rather than flag himself before Martok as the one who spilled the Klingons' guts.

The chance to step back into the shadows showed as pure distaste on Worf's face and in his manner. He probably hadn't wanted to face Martok, but now given the opportunity to slip out, he bucked.

"I would prefer to be there," he said. "I cannot avoid responsibility for what I have done today."

A strange way to phrase it.

Sisko wanted to ask him what he meant, what he felt, and why he felt that way. However, that was no more appropriate than offering apology.

"Call it what you want," he said. "Let's go."

"I must compliment you on your intelligence network, Captain."

General Martok sat lazily in the wardroom and accepted the challenge as Sisko faced him across the table and drummed out his knowledge of the shattering news.

Beside Sisko, Worf sat stiffly.

"One day," Martok went on, "you must tell me how you learned of our plans."

He knew.

Worf tipped a bit forward. "General, I—"

Sisko snapped up a hand. "How I got the information isn't important."

"I think it is," Martok said. "And so will Gowron."

"General," Sisko continued as if uninterrupted, "I want you to call off this attack."

"And what do you propose we do instead?" Martok's voice suddenly boomed. "Stand by and let the Dominion take over the Alpha Quadrant?"

Sisko matched boom for boom. "You have no proof that there are any Founders in Cardassia."

"The change in government is all the proof we need."

"What if you're wrong?" Worf undergirded.

"That would be unfortunate . . . for the Cardassians."

"General," Sisko pursued, "I'd advise you to reconsider. The Federation Council has informed Gowron that if the attack goes forward, it will jeopardize our treaty with the Klingon Empire."

Hit full in the face with that statement, Martok mellowed some and the smugness washed out of his face. "Believe me, Captain, we have no wish to antagonize your people."

"Then call off the attack."

Blunt-struck with facing down the Federation, as if it had never occurred to him that the Federation might stand by its most prickly principles and stand against them in favor of the Cardassians if necessary, Martok seemed to be actually considering Sisko's demand.

Ultimately the Klingon said, "I will consult with Gowron. You will have his decision within the hour."

He pushed to his feet and headed for the exit, pausing for a dangerous glower at Worf. There was no hiding what Worf had done. They had only managed to keep from stating it outright. In the end that would change nothing in Worf's favor.

Glaring at his picture of villainy, Martok's eyes dripped contempt and bitter lack of understanding that a Klingon could do what this Klingon had done.

Worf was rare, Sisko knew, one of these ethnocentric types who actually didn't buy into the gang mentality, yet who must constantly grapple with it. Now he might die for it.

When Martok exited and the door passively gasped closed, Sisko didn't quite relax.

"You're not one of them," he said to Worf. "Don't let them fool you."

Worf looked at him, then at the silent door panel as if there might be solutions etched upon it.

"But they are part of me," he rumbled. "It will be during the next days that I must find out how big a part."

The comm panel buzzed—alert signal from Ops. They needed him. Something was happening.

Rather than key his comm, Sisko ignored it. Piqued, he leaned forward and stared at Worf. His voice was rusty with agitation.

"It's just genetics, Commander," he said. "If we were only our genetics, we could be bacteria. Come with me."

Infuriated with all this, with Worf, with Odo, with all these people who couldn't decide where their loyalties lay, toward those with whom they shared principles or toward others with the same physical form, Sisko plowed the way to Ops.

There he found Dax, Kira, and O'Brien at their stations, but looking at the forward screen.

Dax didn't turn. "Captain, I think you'd better take a look at this."

"Report," Sisko snapped.

"As soon as General Martok beamed back to his ship," she said, "he sent a message to the Klingon fleet. It was just one word. *N'cha.*"

Sisko turned to Worf, and the others did also.

Under their gaze he translated, " 'Begin.' "

Abruptly O'Brien spoke up. "I'm picking up a huge distortion wave in the subspace field. The Klingon ships are going to warp."

"Can you plot their course?" Kira asked.

"Judging from the vector of the subspace disturbance, I'd say their heading is two-six-nine mark zero-three-two."

Gibberish to any but spacefarers, the numbers were clear as handwriting to Sisko. He gritted his teeth through the storm of possible fallouts coming their way.

"Straight for the Cardassian Empire."

CHAPTER
13

THE WARDROOM FELT HOT. Seated around the table, Sisko's officers were a rainbow of experiences and backgrounds from hundreds of light-years across the known galaxy. Human, Trill, Bajoran, Klingon, changeling.

They were a circus, for sure. And it was for him to make sure that *Deep Space Nine* didn't become the middle ring.

"The Federation Council is trying to contact Gowron, but so far, they've had no response. Until they've had a chance to speak with him, we've been ordered not to get involved."

Kira Nerys was extraordinarily sedate, as if somehow all her life she had expected this. "The Bajoran government has agreed to abide by the decisions of the Federation Council," she said, obviously by rote. If she had any other opinion, she kept it to herself.

Julian Bashir looked up at Sisko. Frustration played in his large, expressive eyes, and the pain of what the answer meant was clear in his voice. "So this means we're not going to warn the Cardassians?"

The inhumanity of it scalded them all. Sisko looked down at him and found his face numb with the weight of his responsibility, and the bindings thereon.

Dax bailed him out. "The Klingons are still our allies. If we warn the Cardassians, we'd be betraying them."

"Besides," Miles O'Brien added, "what if the Klingons are right? What if the Dominion has taken over the Cardassian government?"

"If my people wanted to seize control of Cardassia," Odo suggested, "that *is* how they'd do it."

Sisko was about to pound him with a question about how the devil he would know, given that he'd spent a total of about two days with his "people" in his whole existence, but Kira spoke up and kept him from embarrassing Odo for no reason.

"The coup could've happened just as easily without the Founders," she argued. "The Cardassian dissident movement's been gathering strength for years. And with the Obsidian Order out of the way, they might've finally succeeded."

Made sense. It was a flying leap of logic that when a government had a coup, a race from across the galaxy was responsible. The only way the Founders could get here was through the wormhole guarded by DS9, and

Dax had carefully recorded every passage of every ship, its bills of lading, crew manifests, and medical reports.

Of course, this wasn't the Inquisition. Ships did come and go relatively freely, and had for months, because there had been relative quiet for months. The insidious could be among them with the innocent.

Worf spoke up with the voice of someone intimate to the attitudes involved. He seemed troubled more and more by the moment. Still acting like bacteria.

"There are many Klingons who say we have been at peace too long," he said. "That the Empire must expand to survive. Fear of the Dominion only gives my people an excuse to do what they were born to do. To fight . . . and to conquer."

"If they're so eager to fight," Sisko gauged, "who's to say they'll stop at the Cardassians?"

Kira nodded. "Their next target could be anyone . . . even the Federation."

"If I were you," Dax said to her, "I'd be more worried about Bajor." She scanned the people around her. "Think about it. What good does it do for the Klingons to defeat Cardassia if they don't control the wormhole?"

"If my people return to the old ways," Worf agreed, "no one will be safe."

Sisko ground his foot into the carpet. "Then we've got to make sure that doesn't happen."

"How?" O'Brien asked. "The way I see it, we've only got two choices, both of them bad. If we stand by and do nothing, we risk becoming the Klingons' next target. But if we disobey Starfleet's orders and warn the Cardassians, we may end up *starting* our own war with the Klingons."

"Which means we need a third alternative."

They all looked up at him, then at each other, then back at him as if he had one in his pocket.

Hell, he didn't even have a pocket.

"Trust me. You won't regret this. When it comes to keeping warm, nothing beats Vitarian wool undergarments."

Especially if the wearer is very nearly a fish, which you are, my friend Morn, you are.

"And in case you change your mind about the earmuffs, I'll keep them on hold for you!"

As the big alien lumbered out of the shop, Garak wondered when Morn was going to learn not to dominate conversations. Probably never. He was that type.

Oh, well. Another day, another stitch.

Garak pondered his future, with Klingons about the station and rumors of invasion, of collapse in Cardassia—was there a future for him still?

He had for the past years been barely tolerant of existence here, but now, as it was threatened, he began to hunger that it stay. It seemed there would be no going back from exile to a Cardassia that he would enjoy or of whose government he would be part. There were too many who would execute anyone who had ever been in power—that's the way coups played out. All semblance of the old had to be rubbed out, and he was a semblance as well as any. Even worse than some.

He jolted when the comm line chirped—the smallest things were making him jump lately.

Sisko's voice.

"Mr. Garak, I'd like to see you in the wardroom immediately. And bring your tailor's kit."

A tailor's kit in the wardroom. That was a first.

Garak had dreamed in his life of breaking new ground. Today, this would be it. Imagine the thrill of taking measurements in the wardroom. Stunning.

He had long ago stopped trying to anticipate the vagaries of command whim. Sisko might be launching off on some mission of reconnaissance and wish to be dressed like . . . pick an alien. At least it would be one who *did* wear clothing.

Striding through the wardroom door without chiming the entry bells, Garak didn't bother announcing himself, as he had been summoned. He expected to see only Sisko, perhaps with one other person. What faced him as he came into the room was the full complement of the assembled senior staff.

Dax was speaking. "Altogether, we're talking about well over a hundred ships, just in the first wave."

She paused as she and all the others turned to look at Garak.

"I'm sorry," he said, wondering if the summons had been some kind of mistake, an old computer recording fed through by a glitch. "Am I interrupting?"

At the end of the conference table, Sisko stood up. "I'd like to be measured for a suit."

Garak looked around. "Now?"

"Right now."

"But, Captain, I have your measurements—"

"Take them again." He came out from the table and stood where Garak could maneuver. Then he glanced at Dax. "You were saying, Commander?"

Dax spoke clearly, very clearly. "I was saying that between the ground forces and warships, the Klingons have committed almost a third of their military to this invasion."

Sisko turned just enough to see the Klingon in the Starfleet uniform. "How long until they reach their target?"

With an uneasy glance at Garak, the big Klingon seemed irresolute. "According to our estimates, the task force will enter Cardassian space within the hour."

The measuring implements were cold in Garak's hands.

Unless perhaps it was his very skin that had gone cold. He looked at Sisko, and knew that his horror was showing in his face. In Sisko's face shone the truth of it. Sisko was caught between a slothful Federation bureaucracy and the Klingons who weren't being very good allies. And all he had to depend upon was one rather questionable Cardassian exile. He had to obey the letter of the law, but somehow follow its spirit along a different path.

As he glanced up, Garak reminded himself not to let Benjamin Sisko's sedate composure cause any underestimation of the man's boldness.

"Don't forget the waist," Sisko said. "I think I've lost a little weight."

"No, no . . ." Garak gathered his tailor's kit and

stepped back from the large man. "Thank you, Captain. I think I have everything I need."

"Look, I don't care what you've heard about me, and I don't care how long it's been since my communication code has been out of favor. I want to speak to Gul Dukat and I *shall* speak to him. I have critical news. I will get him this news through you this hour or through someone else in the next, and when he discovers that you, his subordinate, failed to put me through, your hide will be the new cover on his flagship's command chair! Put . . . me . . . through!"

His intensity pierced the resistant layers, one by one. Things had certainly changed, for he couldn't even use the same lines of communication on which he had relied in the past.

They had to listen to him. He was holding the bomb in his hands.

"Garak." Gul Dukat's elongated face, a Cardassian face, came onto the screen with a frightening flicker.

Garak was startled with the level of relief that struck him on seeing another Cardassian face. Even if it was Dukat.

"Gul Dukat," he began, and instantly controlled himself. This could play well for him in the future. "I have tantalizing information for you. Only I could get it, I want you to remember."

"Garak, you're wasting my time. You've been on that forsaken knob for years. You're one of them now. Why should I listen to you?"

"You're a rapacious idiot, Dukat. But that won't hurt you anymore. Listen to me. The Klingons are amassing a force with which they intend . . . to invade Cardassia."

Charming! A perfect picture of Dukat, knocked dumb with shock. If only there were a way to freeze it and sell to Quark for marketing.

Dukat's mouth made the word *Klingons* two or three times before he got it out.

"The Klingons? Why would the Klingons invade us?"

"According to my sources, they believe that Cardassia has been taken over by the Founders."

"That's ridiculous!"

A wonderful base-reaction, but Garak gazed at him with unshielded suspicion. Dukat himself could be one of those liquid primordials.

"Is it?" he asked slowly.

"Garak, you've got to talk to Sisko!" Dukat said. *"Tell him he has to find a way to stop the Klingons. Cardassia has enough problems right now!"*

Deviously Garak grinned. "Having trouble keeping the civilians in line?"

Dukat's face flushed deep gray. *"How do you know about that?"*

"I'm afraid after the fall of the Obsidian Order, Cardassian security isn't what it used to be."

"Yes." Dukat matched Garak's sarcasm and threw in a dash of despise. *"Shame about the Order. I suppose there isn't much of a demand for unemployed spies. Looks like you'll be hemming women's dresses for the rest of your life."*

Keeping the grin on his face was a noteworthy battle and Garak believed he failed. Yet how much lay upon winning a joust with Dukat, when their Empire was on the brink of shattering?

"We can sit here all day reminding ourselves of how much we hate each other," he said. "But *you* don't have the time. The Klingon fleet will reach Cardassian territory in less than an hour. So I suggest you get ready for them."

Without signature, he snapped off the communication. Dukat could believe him or not.

He would.

Though such names as "idiot" made fine flinging fodder between the two of them, and "rapacious" even better, Dukat wasn't so much the idiot that he wouldn't read fact where fact lay. Garak didn't ask for restoration of rank, maneuver for favors, or suggest payment. Dukat would notice that.

And as much as he hated to admit the miserable even to himself, he was rooting for Dukat.

Black open space erupted in a string of explosions from here to as far as the sensors could see. Ah, beautiful, the reopening of the Klingon sphere of power.

Martok felt proud, lucky, to be the one orchestrating the rebirth. This was as the universe should be. The strong, the mighty, the bold taking influence which by all right of nature was theirs. There would be a bloodbath first, but that too was nature at work. Wholesale butchery was very often the cost of proper balance.

On his forward screen, white and yellow blooms of disruption flocked from ship after ship as the fleet took the row of outposts here on the Cardassian border.

"Drex." He spoke up, breaking the appreciative silence on his bridge. "Status of the assault on these outposts?"

"All ships reporting success, General," his operations master said. "The outposts are taken."

"I thought so. Tell them to cease fire if possible and conserve their weapons capacity. Prepare to move on to the Cardassian colonies."

"Very good," Drex said with a slight flare.

"So you too are anxious?" Martok looked at him.

"I'm enthused, sir. This will enflame our entire culture as nothing has in half my lifetime."

The fire in the distance had ceased. The long, sparse line of Klingon vessels, stretching far beyond sight or sensor, was dropping off occupying forces onto the outposts, and soon they would be moving on in their single long line to the string of colonies.

"Not the best strategy," Martok uttered.

Drex looked up. "Sir?"

"Just dreaming, Drex. If we had the best of situations, we would have a different strategy." He put his hands together, fingers touching, and made a pointing motion. "We would go in tightly and sharply, in concentration, like a knife. We would thrust straight through to Cardassia Prime, take their homeworld, wrest control from their seat of government, and execute all the political leaders. That's how it's done . . . but we can't do that."

Leaving his controls to come closer to the command center, Drex lowered his voice. "Because of changelings?" he asked quietly.

Martok narrowed his eyes. "They are frightening, aren't they? An enemy who can disguise himself so well. Because we're dealing with them, we have to make a wide-front assault. The only way to find them is to contain them. We must be sure that no ship escapes from Cardassian space. So we come in like this, in a long, long line, and we destroy anything that tries to leave."

Drex nodded, but continued gazing at Martok as if reading a screen. "Sir," he began, "we have never found a single changeling, have we?"

Martok roared back in laughter and smacked his second officer hard on the shoulder. "You know me too well, Drex! I'll have to kill you now!"

And he laughed again. This time Drex laughed a little too, but was still waiting for the answer to his question.

"Not a single one," Martok soon confirmed.

"Perhaps they're hiding. That is something they do better than anything else, after all."

"Or, Drex . . . perhaps there are none."

The sounds of the bridge rippled around them. Others in their crew were occupied with orchestrating the invading force, hurrying about to coordinate incoming reports and send out instructions. But some were canting their heads to listen.

That was all right. Martok wasn't much for secrets. They made him itch.

"No changelings discovered so far," he went on. "And that makes me think."

Shifting his feet on the uneven deck, Drex scratched an old injury on his neck. He always did that when he was confused. "About why the Empire has invaded Cardassia, if there is no visible enemy?"

"Yes. About that. And about why Gowron did not have me destroy *Deep Space Nine* when I had the chance. I thought at first that was why we were going there, you know. Then later I was told otherwise. Surely Gowron knows we will have to get control of the wormhole sector. If what Gowron and the High Council really want is to keep the Dominion out, there is a very simple way. But it's not here, in Cardassian space. It's back there, in Bajoran space. It's sitting in space right next to that infernal Federation pile of bolts."

For a few moments Drex said nothing. His eyes were tight with concentration, his mouth twisted as he sifted for what Martok was implying.

Abruptly his eyes changed and he sucked in a breath. "Destroy the wormhole!"

"Yes," Martok congratulated. "Burn the only bridge. Therefore, why didn't we?"

Placing one hand thoughtfully upon the arm of the command chair, Drex turned to look out over the string of outposts that guarded the border no longer for the Cardassians but now for the Klingons.

"I don't know . . . then what is the real reason for this invasion?" he murmured aloud. Then, quite sharply, he looked at Martok again. "Pure conquest?"

"It tastes good, doesn't it?" Martok watched realization bloom in his officer's face. "Yes . . . to make sure the sword of Klingon does not rust. There may be a danger of the Founders coming through the wormhole and spreading here, but so far I have seen no evidence. Do you think Gowron is that bright, Drex? I don't know . . . possibly. If so, then I respect him for this plot. The Cardassians are like us in many ways. Sneakier, less honorable, but certainly not likely to coddle spineless races the way the Federation does. Thus, perhaps war between us and Cardassia is inevitable, and in this case, it is perfect."

"How so? Our supply lines are long, the Federation is unhappy with us—"

"Those are small concessions. What difference does it make ultimately what the Federation 'thinks' of us?"

"None, I suppose."

"No, none at all. Look at the whole picture. We have an enemy with no face. We can blame him for anything that happens. An imaginary foe with whom we can saddle any accident. Whole massacres can be justified in an instant. Destruction is being taken to the Cardassians' home space, and we still have the advantage of surprise. Though Cardassia will have the advantage of shorter supply lines, Cardassian property will take all the damage. Our home territories will remain untouched. Our production facilities will continue to produce. Our children will be safe in their beds, to become the next generation of warriors. And our warriors will finally have an outlet for all their training. It is a sublime plan . . . and I am comfortable with it."

Together they gazed at the main screen's view of flickering space, but in their minds they saw other things. Whatever was about to happen, and whatever the reason, they were both suddenly invigorated.

No longer would Klingons bow to the quiescence of the Federation, but they would follow their instincts and do what Klingons must do.

Song, wine, women, and war. What else was there? Now they would have all those.

"Sir," Drex began tentatively, "what if the Dominion really is a threat?"

"In time, Drex, in good time," the general answered. "If my guess is right and the High Council is smarter than they act, then the Gamma Quadrant is in their sights also. First we take Cardassia, as is only natural. The weakling Federation will never stand up to us against those reptiles. One by one we will slip into new systems, always following the ghost of changelings. Eventually, even the Federation will buckle. Nothing lasts forever, you know."

"Yes . . ."

"And after the Alpha Quadrant is all Klingon, what next?"

"Through the wormhole . . ."

"Of course. That must be why Gowron didn't have us attack the station when we had the chance. That's why we left the wormhole intact . . . not for the Dominion, but for ourselves."

"But the changelings . . . they *are* there."

"Even they are not gods, Drex. Our science will find some way to beat them. Once we find out how to do that, we can take the Gamma Quadrant too. No more subservience, Drex . . . no more sniveling. And you and I, we shall be at the forefront of it all as it unfolds. The light of history will shine upon my name as the offensive general of it all, and your name will glow beside mine. This ship will become the symbol of victory. Warriors will dream of serving on it and children will play with models of it. Think of that!"

He laughed again, and slapped Drex again.

"General," the helm officer interrupted, "all Cardassian outposts are staffed with occupying forces, and the fleet is ready to advance now."

"Very well. All ships, coordinate position and go to warp factor six. Destination, the Cardassian colonies in Sector Two. We will be in the lead."

He glanced at Drex, and Drex smiled.

"What is our estimated arrival time at the colonies?"

"Approximately four hours at warp six, General," Drex told him.

"General." The communications and sensors officer turned from his position on the upper left bridge. "A message is coming in from Chancellor Gowron."

"Personal?"

"No, sir. I have the message now."

"Relay it."

"He is coming to this sector . . . will rendezvous with you at the Cardassian colonies . . . prepare for glory."

Martok felt the smile wither from his face. "Acknowledge that," he grunted. Pressing back in his chair he frowned. "He comes to snatch away the credit from us. By being here with us, he steals our prominence. That government fungus! Drex, I have no idea why anyone would want to claw and scratch and maneuver for a lifetime to get on the High Council. These families who suffer and twist to get a member on the Council—why? What does it really get them in the end? They sit in stuffy chambers, bickering and croaking, then go into a closed court and practice with their rusty *bat'leth*s and think that makes them Klingon. Why? So all of them can pretend they're ready to go out and do what I have spent a career doing! Jealous! Now Gowron comes here so my light will shine on him."

"But there's nothing we can do," Drex said. "We can only hope he doesn't try to take *all* the credit."

"If he tries," Martok said, "I shall have to do something about it."

Ops. A dim world of flickering indicator lights and the shadows that defined them. The heart of *Deep Space Nine.* More—the heart of this very crucial sector.

Against the canvas of deepest, darkest, emptiest space, Worf stood with strangers and watched eternity unroll.

On the Ops display table, where O'Brien told him there was usually a station diagram, now shone a star chart of the Cardassian/Bajoran border. Graphics blotted off the Cardassian systems that had already been overrun by the Klingons—all the systems closest to that border.

No one spoke in the room. From the direction of his office Captain Sisko's low voice warbled unintelligibly as he spoke to someone on a monitor.

Not just someone . . . the Federation Council.

He was a man of duty, this Sisko. He would use subterfuge when he needed to, as all border guards had learned to do, but when the shoving began he would do so under orders, and with the sanction of those with whom he had those principles in common.

Sisko knew where his line was drawn. Worf found himself plied with envy.

Leaning over the star charts, Major Kira was as intent as if it were her own world and not her lifetime enemy being overrun by conquerors. Worf watched, and he envied her too.

"Based on Klingon transmissions we've intercepted," she was saying, "the outlying Cardassian colonies were overrun almost immediately. But now that the Cardassian fleet has mobilized, the Klingons are meeting stronger resistance."

Wryly, Dax said, "Mmm . . . you'd almost think someone warned the Cardassians they were coming."

No one even acknowledged her joke.

"Hopefully," Kira went on, "this will make the Klingons think twice about what they're doing."

"Unlikely, Major." Worf spoke up for the first time in half an hour. "Now that the battle has begun, Martok and his troops will settle for nothing less than victory."

They looked at him as if wondering why he hadn't said that before, and he looked back at them, wondering why they hadn't assumed it all along.

They fell silent as Sisko left his office and joined them, his posture and expression unreadable.

Seconds ticked off, then O'Brien piped, "Well? What did the Federation Council say?"

Sisko verbally shrugged. "They've decided to condemn the Klingon invasion."

No one was surprised, yet everyone reacted.

"In response," Sisko went on, "Gowron has expelled all Federation citizens from the Klingon Empire and recalled the ambassadors back from the Federation."

Kira narrowed her eyes. "You're saying he's cut off diplomatic relations?"

"He's done more than that," Sisko said. He looked at each of them, but somehow when all was done he ended up looking at Worf. "The Klingons have withdrawn from the Khitomer Accords. The peace treaty between the Federation and the Klingon Empire . . . has ended."

PART
THREE

PART
THREE

CHAPTER
14

"CAPTAIN, YOU'RE NEVER going to believe this."

Chief O'Brien stood his station almost casually, but Worf realized the engineer was attempting to offset the tension in what he had to say.

"A Klingon ship just decloaked off upper pylon three and is requesting permission to dock. They claim Chancellor Gowron is on board and is demanding to speak with Mr. Worf. Personally."

Worf frowned as he found himself again at the core of a crisis he thought he had shifted away from. He'd done his duty, performed his tricky task, put himself in the light of contempt and interstellar espionage, and handed the weight back to his commanding officer, where it belonged. As he met Captain Sisko's eyes, he knew those barbells were about to be handed back to him.

"Extend docking clamps, Mr. O'Brien," Sisko said, "but tell them to stay on board their ship until I give them clearance. This is a potential diplomatic rupture and they're going to have to wait."

"They're taking a hell of a chance!" Kira reckoned as she checked the weapons integrity of the Klingon ship and made sure they weren't about to shoot. "With the treaty dead, what's a Klingon high official doing in Federation space?"

"We could arrest him," Dax suggested. "We could arrest the whole crew."

Kira looked at Sisko. "Or we could fire on them and be completely within our options. Either they're allies with us or they're not! They can't have it both ways!"

O'Brien gave a semiapproving shrug. "Might be interesting to find out why the chancellor himself would come all this way under a collapsing treaty, just to talk to one specific person."

Ben Sisko had listened to all this in measuring silence, gauging his options. Now moving to Worf, he pressed one hand to the Ops table and kept his voice low.

"You'll have to talk to him, Mr. Worf. I won't order you to go aboard the Klingon vessel. Not yet at least. I can make a counterrequest that Gowron come on board the station and say what he has to say to both of us."

A moment ago, Worf had resisted the idea of going on board the Klingon vessel under these conditions, even Gowron's vessel. Among Klingons, hatred for him might be running high at this moment. He might have to fight his way past every guard who had heard of his service in Starfleet instead of the Klingon military and now perhaps of his questioning of Klingon command. They all suspected he wouldn't lie quiet in favor of those things now.

"It could be plain vengeance," Sisko evaluated. "You could be walking into murder. Your own."

"Gowron will not allow that," Worf said, clasping his hands behind him. "We are close friends. But they could use me as a hostage, and you would be in that vise. Yet if I fail to appear, cowardice will glaze my name and all of Starfleet. The first step in the Federation's part of this conflict would be a backward one."

Sisko paused and thought his way through what Worf had just said. "What's your history with Gowron? Why would he protect you? I can't believe even friendship is enough when they want so much to incite a war."

"Gowron helped restore my honor when I had lost it. He and I have made . . . investments in each other."

Worf didn't look at Sisko, but gazed only at the star chart on the table, and at the open air. He hoped Sisko didn't demand to know the details of those investments, for such things were exclusive between warriors and not fodder for conversation.

But Sisko, as he stood shoulder to shoulder with Worf, almost the same mass of body and almost the same height, didn't press further for details.

Instead he folded his arms and said, "I'm willing to twist that around and require Gowron to take the risks. Order him to come here to meet you."

"It may indeed be a risk," Worf appraised, "but the Klingon fleet will not see it that way, sir. Word spreads quickly. We must appear undaunted before Gowron. I am willing to go on board his ship."

"All right," Sisko said, "then consider yourself under orders to go. And it'll be on me if anything goes wrong."

Worf squared his shoulders and came almost to attention. "I would rather take the responsibility, sir."

Sharply Sisko refuted. "It's not yours to take. Prepare to go aboard."

Gowron. Chancellor of the Klingon High Council. Ruler of the Klingon Empire. A height that Worf, as an officer in Starfleet, had never expected to scale, but he had scaled it before Gowron had himself reached that level.

Now Worf stood on the promontory as well, escorted to the bridge of the Klingon flagship as it reposed like a spider at the docking ring of *Deep Space Nine*. He was still technically in Federation territory, docked to a Federation station, well away from the shattering border of Cardassian/Bajoran space, and yet he might as well have been standing on the Klingon home planet of Qo'nos, so removed was he from the safety of those with whom he had deeper things in common.

Dax could pull him back at a touch of his comm badge, but even that wouldn't be soon enough if things went wrong.

Gowron had been his friend in the past, but things change. Impending war could make loyalties shudder, and there was already a gulf between the two of them—Worf served Starfleet, not the Klingon fleet, and that would remain wedged between them.

The bridge door opened before him and his two Klingon escorts stepped aside. He moved into the sorrel lighting, where Gowron was conferring with the bridge crew of his ship.

Gowron looked up. His triangular face and blazing blue eyes set in the frame of wild hair and a monk's untended beard stood out instantly among the other Klingons.

Especially those eyes. Big as fists.

"Chancellor Gowron," Worf began, his own deep voice bludgeoning the bridge with new sound. "You wished to speak with me."

He expected trouble, and thus was taken aback when Gowron's face broke into untimely delight and his tone reveled with welcome.

"Worf! It is good to see you."

Pushing back his robes, the chancellor crossed the deck to embrace Worf. Then he drew back and surveyed Worf with critical affection.

"I always said that uniform would get you in trouble someday."

"It seems you were right," Worf accommodated, careful not to show weakness by glancing at the other officers in the crew, but to fix his gaze only on Gowron as if not even tempted to look elsewhere. "But I will not apologize for my—"

"Yes, yes. I know you did what you thought was right. And even though you may have made some enemies, I assure you I am not one of them."

Relief piled through Worf and his stomach lost

some of its knots. "I am glad. Your friendship means much to me."

"And yours to me. It has been too long since you last fought at my side. But now the time has come again. We will do great deeds in the coming days. Deeds worthy of song."

Song? What would happen if the events played out as they were set? There would be no one left who felt much like singing.

Worf stared at him. Had they risked coming all the way here, just to ask one more warrior to join them?

He waited for Gowron to laugh and say he was making a joke.

"You want me to go with you to Cardassia?" Worf asked him, swarmed with sudden, unexpected temptation.

Gowron spread his arms.

"What better way to redeem yourself in the eyes of your people? Come with me, Worf . . . glory awaits you on Cardassia!"

CHAPTER
15

"WORF, WHY DO you stand there like a mute *d'blok?* I have offered you a chance for glory. All you have to do is take it!"

Take it. Snatch back the illusive respect of a people who gave respect but sparingly. Take on a silver plate the utter fame that would be his as the only Klingon to serve in Starfleet who then abandoned Starfleet and came to fight at the side of Gowron during the great war against the Dominion-possessed Cardassians.

Yes, it was a song after all.

But he did not *believe.* When the sweat and stink of battle rose around him in its dizzying cloud, he would be laden by his own lack of allegiance to anything the Klingons had ever stood for as a race. They raised the chalice in their own recognition, but what was the color of the wine?

That empty chalice hit him with all its contents as he looked into Gowron's wild blue eyes. To be mindlessly Klingon was not enough.

"If there is glory to be won," he said slowly, "it will have to be yours alone." His mouth went dry and the next words were a struggle as he heard ringing in his mind all that he was giving up. "I cannot come with you, Gowron."

Pure shock rolled across the chancellor's face. That anyone could disagree with him was a complete mystery to him. He saw his way, and his way was all. He had ironed out his logic and was blunted that anyone could think differently. A chance for glory embedded within a chance to trample down the Dominion—how could there be any other choice?

"Of course you can," he insisted, gesturing at the bridge around them as if it were all of Klingon. "It is where you belong!"

Worf felt at a loss having to explain that which should be clear to anyone who wore any kind of uniform, the symbol of a devotion and a cause.

"I cannot abandon my post," he said simply.

"You no longer have a post!" Gowron flashed across the bridge, waving his hands now. "You have no place on that station! And no business wearing that uniform!"

"I have sworn an oath of allegiance—"

"With the Federation!" Gowron spat the word as if it had no flavor, no substance. As if an oath to the Federation were an oath to nothing.

Worf stared at him in disbelief. "You would have me break my word?"

They stared at each other, dumbfounded at the

tenor of this conversation. Worf had always considered Gowron his friend and Gowron obviously thought the same, to risk coming all the way here with no treaty just to pick Worf up for the fight. In Gowron's mind he was doing Worf a fabulous favor and couldn't imagine having it turned down.

They were realizing something bitter as they gazed at each other. Their points of view were entirely incompatible. Until war came, they hadn't found that out.

"Your word?" Gowron growled. "What good is your word when you give it to people who care nothing for honor? Who refuse to lift a finger while Klingon warriors shed blood for *their* protection! I tell you, they are without honor!" He bolted closer, and his tone changed to a fume. "And you do not owe them anything."

"It is not what I owe them that matters," Worf contested. "It is what I owe myself. Worf, son of Mogh, does not go against his oath."

Gowron was unimpressed, still stunned by the turn of choices. He placed a hand on his chest.

"And what of your debt to me? I gave you back your name, gave your family a seat on the High Council. And this . . . is how you repay me?"

Worf met his glare boldly, without flinch. "It is true I owe you a great debt. I would give my life for you. But invading Cardassia is wrong and I cannot support it."

Gowron went abruptly cold. He saw the pillar before him and knew it could not be swayed. His manner changed, though he boiled beneath the surface. He paced the bridge, catching glances with his crew, and Worf realized that Gowron had risked not only his life and his ship, but his own honor to come here into Federation space.

And now he was on the verge of losing the respect of these men who looked at him now, if he failed to bring this vagrant warrior back to the fold.

"Worf," he began again, "I have always considered you a friend and an ally. And because you are my friend, I am giving you this one last chance to redeem yourself. Come with me."

Worf stood firm. "I cannot."

With monumental strength Gowron remained calm. "Think about what you're doing," he suffered. "If you turn your back on me now, for as long as I live you will not be welcome anywhere in the Klingon Empire. Your family will be removed from the High Council, your lands seized, and your House stripped of its titles. You will be left with nothing."

If Gowron had yelled, shouted, growled, harped these threats, they would have been only that. But he spoke with resigned commitment and the stamina of knowing what was coming for his civilization. To be Klingon was all, for Gowron.

Worf envied him in that moment, to be able to rattle off such personal destruction with resolve. Distaste filled him for a culture that impales the group for the commitments of one.

He stood even straighter, and looked without shudder into Gowron's eyes.

"Nothing except my honor," he said.

He thought it would be a hard thing to say, but it wasn't. He knew more what he wanted than even he had comprehended until this moment. Redemption had been handed him on a platter, and he was turning it down.

Gowron narrowed those spooky eyes, then accepted that two strong-minded individuals had reached their impasse. He had humiliated himself before his crew and word would spread.

"So be it."

And he turned away from Worf. And he did not look at him again.

"Open fire."

The hull of the *Negh'Var* shuddered very slightly as full-powered disruptor energy tore away from its weapons ports and blanketed the space around the Cardassian colony below.

The feeble defense shields put up by the colony were already crumbling and the Klingon fleet had only been here five minutes. This would be easier than Martok expected.

Still, he enjoyed shouting the order to fire. There was something thrilling about that.

"Colonial shields are down," Drex reported. "Their defense runabouts are retreating. Reports are coming in from other vessels in our fleet. Similar situations. Eleven colonies already subjugated, ten more collapsing at predicted rates."

"Good, very good . . . send in an occupying force, no more than twenty men. And someone go and get my breakfast. Battle makes me hungry."

"Yes, General." Drex turned and made a gesture at the low-ranking officer at the engineering station, who nodded and rushed toward the turbolift.

"Drex, instruct the *Lechraj*, the *Rok*, the *Vortacha*,

and the *Mu'Gor* to establish headquarters on their colonial possessions immediately and return to formation and prepare to advance on Cardassia Prime. And tell that weasel Koru that I expect a *full* accounting of his disruptor consumption this time. No more of his games."

"Yes, General."

"We must capture the Detepa Council members if we are to collapse the Cardassian government with any efficiency. I want to do that today. No sense waiting."

"Yes, General."

"If we take over Cardassia Prime quickly, then the Federation will be less likely to interfere. They will send diplomats and negotiators instead of fighting ships and they will try to talk us away. While they talk, we will entrench ourselves deeper and deeper into the Cardassian system and before long there will be nothing more to talk about. Then we will kick them out too."

Drex rewarded him wiht a supportive nod. "Very exciting plan, sir."

"I like long-range plans," Martok sighed hungrily. "The future is a beautiful tunnel. . . . Where are those four ships? What's taking them so long? Why were transporters invented if not to hurry up occupations?"

"They are coming now," Drex said from his position at the tactical computer. *"Vortacha* is lingering behind. They've taken some damage to their aft thrusters. Repairs under way."

"They can repair as we go. Come about, one-two-eight mark four, formation *RoChaq'Va.* Destination

Cardassia Prime. Warp factor six as soon as we clear the asteroid field."

Drex nodded, and this time smiled. "Understood."

Yes, his second officer understood perfectly well. There was reason to Martok's rush. He wanted to get to Cardassia Prime and smash the government before Gowron had a chance to rendezvous with him and share the credit.

"*Vortacha* signals ready to advance, General," Drex reported, then added, "Asteroid field is dead ahead."

"Warp factor two around the field."

"Yes, General," the helm officer responded, and pressed the *Negh'Var* into motion.

The asteroid field was a shimmering wall of stones caught in the local star's and each other's gravity, and whose accompanying dust and collected debris veiled any attempt to see through it, even with sensors. Therefore it held a certain enthralling mystery, as some things in space still did.

Martok sat back to enjoy what he was seeing, and to wallow in imaginings of what was soon to come. His fleet was strong, his conquests going as numbered, and he thought he had figured out the real future. There would now be conquest for him, for his four sons, and for the son to whom his daughter had just given birth. The Empire's destiny, so long put off by the unexpected expansion of the United Federation of Planets, would finally play out. The galaxy was shining before him, for soon it would be Klingon.

The asteroid field lowered slowly to the bottom of the main screen as the *Negh'Var* led the other ships over the top of the large stones and skirted the veil of shimmering dust. As they came over it they would adjust their vectors and increase speed to cover quickly the light-years between here and Cardassia Prime. And on Cardassia Prime, people were having their peaceful meals and never expecting what was about to come.

Perhaps not so peaceful for some—they had just endured a revolution, of course. Upheaval could be so inconvenient.

He was getting very hungry. What was taking so long with that breakfast?

"General . . ." Drex gazed into his screens, hunched over until his face was only inches from the console.

Martok tipped his head in that direction, but didn't really bother moving. "Something?"

"A distortion in subspace . . . I'm not sure . . ."

"Well? What is it?"

"The dust is causing some distortion, but I believe I'm picking up . . . an exhaust reading." Drex adjusted his controls, shook his head, frowned, then adjusted again. "Possibly residue from ships that passed through here in the past day . . ."

"Is it or isn't it?"

"I cannot be certain. The dust—"

"Is only dust, Drex. Do your job."

"Yes, sir. . . . I do read some solid shadows . . . beyond the asteroid field and on the lower plane." Drex raised his head to the main screen and watched as they came up over the asteroids' rim of dust. "We should be able to see in a moment if there is anything there."

"Weapons officer, put one bank on-line and prepare

to wreck whatever we see. Some unlucky trader, most likely."

"Ready, General," the weapons officer said.

"Be sure you leave no recognizable debris. I want to be seen as a conqueror, not as a pirate."

"Yes, General."

Casually the *Negh'Var* maneuvered over the wide-girthed wall of asteroids, with the brown sea floating under it in uneven waves. Pebbles crackled on its outer hull plates, ringing through the structure of the ship and creating a strange little music.

Martok smiled at Drex as they listened to the sound. They found it pleasant to have some contact with the outside, something spacefarers cherished for they had so little of that.

As they came up over the asteroids and finally cleared the veil of dust, they leaned forward a little as the ship angled downward and prepared to set itself to the correct vector for high warp to its destination.

Martok scanned the spacescape for the ship that had been tickling their sensors, but there was nothing nearby.

Then the helmsman turned the ship deeper into the proper heading, and the main screen picked up a string of solid objects.

"What are those?" Martok snapped. "Maximum magnification—hurry up."

"Maximum magnification," the helm officer repeated, and adjusted his controls.

Martok surged out of his chair.

"Cardassians!"

Scarcely was the sound out of his throat than the

row of—how many were there?—ten or twelve Cardassian Galor-class warships opened up on them, all firing at once.

The *Negh'Var* was blistered by a torrent of raw disruptor fire suddenly tethering the two fleets together in a hideous dance.

As the deck tilted under them, Martok and his crew were pitched on their heads. Bones cracked and blood splattered. Only six of the ten bridge crew crawled back toward their posts.

"Shields! Shields!" Martok croaked, desperate, but there was no one at the defense position to put the shields up. "Drex! Where are you?"

Through a billow of greenish electrical smoke his second's voice was shaky. "Here . . . here, General . . ."

"The shields! Put them up!"

"I'm trying to reach them."

"Return fire immediately! Tell the other ships to do the same! And call the fleet from the colonies! Bring reinforcements!"

"The Cardassians are blocking our transmissions, General." The outline of Drex shone foggily through the smoke, huddling over the defense-systems grid.

Martok pawed for the helm. "All ships, disperse! Draw them apart!"

"I can't reach the other ships in our formation either."

Reaching down, Martok found his helm officer and pulled the dazed man back into his seat. "Swing wide! They'll have to decipher our actions and make decisions for themselves."

"Yes, sir," the helm officer coughed.

"General!" Drex called over the crackling of shattered systems howling through the ship. "Our shield generator is off-line. Engineering wants your permission to sacrifice weapons power long enough to recharge."

"Yes! What choice do we have? Evasive action!"

They were hit again, cudgeled by a great hand of energy pumped from the Cardassian fleet.

During this moment, in which he could do nothing but glare in hatred at what he saw on the screen, at the row of Cardassian warships closing in on them and at his own advance fleet being grazed by strokes of disruptor power, he grasped the helm chair before him and ground his teeth.

"They knew we were coming!" he gnashed. "They were ready for us! They were *ready* for us!"

Another javelin of energy sliced through space and blistered the bare underside of the ship as the helm officer desperately tried to evade the onrushing Cardassians. Without shields, and unable to make a counterstrike while sacrificing weapons to recharge the shields, they would soon be shredded.

All his plans, shredded! All the golden possibilities, wrecked!

"We have to survive," he growled. "We have to get through them! Everything depends on it!"

"They're closing in, General," Drex said, then paused to cough harshly. In the middle of a cough he looked up sharply and choked, "Sir, new contact!"

"More Cardassians?"

"No—sir, it is the *Prakesh!* Chancellor Gowron's ship! Coming in very fast!"

"Gowron! I forgot all about him! Clear the way! Let

him in!" Martok shoved his helm officer aside and clawed at the controls himself.

In a sickening maneuver the deck dropped out from under them as the pummeled ship ducked away and let Gowron's vessel plow in and take the onslaught of a half dozen Cardassian warships.

On its flickering shields Gowron's ship took the blasting meant to shatter the *Negh'Var.* Confronted with a full-powered ship, the Cardassian assault formation broke up and split off in several directions; then two of those ships vectored back to continue hammering Gowron.

That gave Martok a chance to skim back over the asteroid field and gain time to recharge those shields.

"Aft view!" he shouted.

Someone on the bridge complied, and the main screen shifted to show Gowron's ship being crushed between the disruptor beams of two Galor-class ships.

"Drex! Hurry with those shields! We have to go back!"

"Nearly ready, General."

"Turn back. You—get back in your seat!" He grabbed the helm officer again and stuffed him back at his post, then twisted toward the weapons station and shouted, "Prepare to open fire! We have to get them out of there! I don't want to be obliged to him!"

With its shields up but still fickle against the blasting energy from the scattered Cardassian ships, *Negh'Var* turned to the face of the enemy. They opened fire and at least provided some element of confusion in which the smoldering *Prakesh* could be protected.

One Cardassian ship angled away and bore straight at the *Vortacha,* which had not yet had a chance to repair its thrusters and couldn't maneuver out of the way.

In seconds, a ball of radiant energy bloomed where there had been a ship.

Then two other Klingon vessels came in and repaid the Cardassians by turning three of their ships into fireboxes. The Cardassian assault line tried to reassemble, but by now two more Klingon ships were coming up over the asteroid field and throwing their weight into the chaotic battle. Ships began to pair off, grazing each other with superheated energy and biting at each other's power centers.

That would be how this fight would go—fleets nearly matched in numbers would pound at each other until the balance went off, and those with more ships left would be able to gain advantage.

Already the Cardassian defense fleet was being cut up. But there was a cost—the Klingon fleet was losing ships, and even more critical, they had lost their element of surprise. Cardassia Prime was suddenly out of reach.

As Martok watched the *Prakesh* boil with smoke, obviously heavily damaged and losing atmosphere in great silvery funnels from at least four sections, he realized how deeply their attack plans had been compromised. The surprise had been crucial, and now that was gone.

"Have you broken through the interference yet?" he snapped toward his upper deck. "Can you contact Gowron?"

"I will try, sir . . ." the communications officer wheezed. He had only one working arm, but he still stood his post.

In a few seconds, Gowron's wild-eyed face appeared on the crackling main screen.

"This is Gowron. . . . You will beam me and my survivors aboard. This ship's main warp core is breached."

"Very well," Martok complied, with a glance at Drex. Having Gowron on board his own ship was not particularly desirable. Then it would become Gowron's ship.

"So you let yourself be surprised, Martok. Shameful."

"It is not I who should be ashamed, Chancellor," Martok defied. "This Cardassian fleet was not out here on some kind of chance maneuvers. They were waiting for us. You ordered me to go to *Deep Space Nine,* and then you went there yourself. We should never have gone anywhere near that place. Sisko has found out our plan and he has betrayed us! He told the Cardassians we were coming! Starfleet is no longer our ally!"

"That means the Detepa officials are expecting us and are probably moving to escape our advancing fleet," Gowron said. *"As soon as we battle down these Cardassians, you will send four ships immediately to Sector Three! If the council members try to escape, they'll head for the first friendly outpost, and that is Deep Space Nine. We must head them off!"*

Alone at the railing again. Below where he sat on the second level of Quark's, the first level was boisterous and bustling. The Klingon task force was gone from the sector, the flagship was gone from the docking ring, and it seemed these people took that absence as a signal to relax, as if Gowron and the other Klingons had taken with him all their troubles.

The war, if there would be war, was happening far enough away, and any hollow became an oasis.

Yes, there would be war. There already was.

Worf looked down from his perch, wishing he could retire to his quarters without making his own absence as obvious as that of the other Klingons'. He took no comfort in the free-breathing of the people below him.

"You look like you could use some company."

O'Brien approached him with a mug in one hand, and sat down with him.

Had O'Brien been asking a question, Worf would have said no, he didn't want anyone to share in his rainy mood, but since his former shipmate didn't ask, Worf was freed from having to suggest staying alone. He was caught between the image he wanted to portray and the needs of his qualmish heart.

"Chief," he began, "do you remember the time we rescued Captain Picard from the Borg?"

O'Brien looked at him as if he had gone mad to have to ask. Then he seemed to understand it was just bar talk, just Worf's way of head-firsting into a conversation.

"How could I forget?" the engineer said. "That was touch and go for a while. Truth is, there were a couple of moments when I thought we were all going to wind up 'assimilated.'"

"I never doubted the outcome," Worf admitted.

"We were like warriors from the ancient sagas. There was nothing we couldn't do."

"Except keep the holodecks working right."

O'Brien smiled, and managed to swerve away from just about the ugliest episode they had in common.

Wondering if the ancient sagas had been embellished over time, Worf thought about how that story would change as it was told and told through the ages. It needed no change at all, but it would change. Everything did.

He felt O'Brien's prodding eyes. The chief knew something was wrong. Or more wrong than before, perhaps. The silent question rattled between them, with O'Brien wise enough to know not to verbalize what he was thinking. He was getting his message across perfectly well, and Worf felt the truth slip out.

"I have decided," he murmured, "to resign from Starfleet."

He tried to speak strongly, but doubted he had succeeded.

The smile fell from O'Brien's face. "Resign? What are you talking about?"

"I have made up my mind. It is for the best."

"Look . . . I know how much you miss the *Enterprise*, but I'm sure they'll be building a new one soon."

"It will not be the same," Worf sharply told him. "The *Enterprise* I knew is gone. And perhaps that is for the better. Those were good years. But it is time for me to move on."

"And do what?" O'Brien pursued, as if he were not sitting in the heart of his own personal alternative to starship duty.

"I don't know," Worf confessed. "I thought I would be returning to Boreth . . . but now that's impossible. I have made an enemy of Gowron. And of every other Klingon in the Empire."

O'Brien offered a small shrug. "All the more reason to stay in Starfleet."

A collective howl erupted below as someone won at the Dabo table, and for a moment the two held silence. The conversation seemed simple enough, but there was a complex burden about it that they both felt intensely. O'Brien's easy face was now troubled, and Worf felt bad that he had put the trouble there. He hadn't wanted to shift his problems to the few friends he had left in the universe.

"This uniform," he continued thoughtfully, "will only serve as a reminder of how I have disgraced myself in the eyes of my people. I suppose I could get a berth on a Nyberrite Alliance cruiser . . . they're always eager to hire experienced officers."

"Nyberrite Alliance," O'Brien uttered, his expression crimping. "That's a long way from anywhere."

"That is my intention."

O'Brien cupped one hand around his mug and made a gesture with the other. "What about your son?"

Melancholy struck Worf full in the face, delivered to the bull's-eye by another father—one who also was separated from his wife and child most of the time.

He had hoped no one would think to speak openly of Alexander. He had hoped to banish those thoughts, of how ghostly a parent he had been nearly the boy's whole life.

"Alexander," he answered, "is much happier living with his grandparents on Earth than he ever was staying with me. One thing is certain—the sooner I leave here, the better. My continued presence on *Deep Space Nine* would only be a liability to Captain Sisko in his dealings with the Klingons."

O'Brien sat back and frowned, a kind of defiant frown that communicated well enough that he didn't care, and knew Sisko didn't care, what the Klingons thought. They'd deal with what came their way, and let fall the chips, without considering putting any individual off the station because it might make things one or two degrees "easier."

Worf was appreciating that silent lecture from O'Brien when a demonic face pressed between them and Worf sat back, startled out of his thoughts.

"Do you hear that, Chief? Seventy-two decibels! Music to my ears."

"I don't know, Quark," O'Brien said, also shifting back an inch or two. "I think I liked it better when it was quiet."

"You want it quiet? Go to the Replimat. This is Quark's the way it should be. The way it was meant to be. Am I glad we finally got rid of all those Klingons."

Quark took a cleansing breath, and found himself staring at Worf.

"Present company excepted, of course," he said, but the damage was done.

Worf had heard such things all his life, but wasn't in the mood to tolerate them from this weasel. He got up and started away.

As he moved off he heard O'Brien say, "That's what

I like about you, Quark. You really know how to make your customers feel welcome."

The scrape of O'Brien's chair followed, and behind that, faintly, Quark's voice was the last thing Worf heard as he left the bar—"Ah, what do I care. All he ever drinks is prune juice."

The settled halls of *Deep Space Nine* were markedly brighter without the dimming presence of Klingons, and that made Worf uneasy. That Klingons should be so dreaded, held in empty contempt because of some common behaviors—it was . . . shallow. But this perception was not the fault of the perceivers. The Klingons generally did behave rudely, were demanding and pushy. That was no one's fault but the Klingons' themselves.

His strides were strong and determined, almost all of the same length as he angled around people and through archways, because he knew that if he paused, he might stop.

He went straight to Benjamin Sisko's office door, and there he stared at the gray panel for nearly ten seconds before touching off the door chimes.

A few seconds later, the door slid away. He pushed himself inside.

Sisko was at his desk.

Worf stepped in about two feet, then stood at attention, not meeting the captain's eyes. "Sir, forgive me for disturbing you. May I have a brief audience?"

"Of course, Commander. Come in." When Worf moved farther in and the door panel closed behind him, the sedate governor of DS9 and its hot sector gestured at the chair in front of his desk. "Sit down."

"I would rather stand, sir."

"Oh?" Sisko could easily have pointed out how rude that was, but he seemed to instantly pick up that this wasn't just another situation report. "Go ahead, Mr. Worf."

"I believe I have reached a decision," Worf forced out unevenly. "A deck officer of my background is always in demand for merchant fleets, and my usefulness has served out in Starfleet, especially under these conditions."

"I see," Sisko responded. He leaned back and knitted his fingers. "Commander . . . as long as you're ditching your career, why don't you get it off your chest and tell me why? Go ahead. I'm a good listener."

Now Worf met the other man's dark eyes and realized that it was true. He *was* a good listener.

Somehow Sisko had divined that perhaps Worf would be helped by hearing out what he was thinking. Could he talk to a mirror? Could he stand on a hilltop and howl his questions to the wind?

Sisko was smart. It was better to speak, if only to provide his commanding officer a genuine panorama of why a good serviceman with experience and a clear record would break off his career just before his civilization might very well need him.

"I feel . . . the eyes of Federation citizens," Worf began with some effort. "They do not know whether or not they can trust me. I do not blame them . . . Klingons have a violent streak. It seems . . . I have it too."

And he lowered his gaze. Perhaps it was because he thought he was going off to the farthest reach of the known galaxy to disappear, but he suddenly didn't care who heard his thoughts. Or it might be Sisko's easy manner, one that said they were alike, men banished to deep space.

His fists curled into knots. His arms went tight. He paced away from the desk. His inner tortures bristled, and for a rare moment he opened up.

"Why must it be," he smoldered, "that Klingons are welcome nowhere but in Klingon space, on Klingon ships, among Klingon kind? What are we—what am *I*—that there must be hostility?"

"Genetic?" Sisko assisted softly. "Fighting genes? I'd like to see *those* under a microscope."

Worf snapped him a look. "It is very difficult to deny your genetics," he simmered, with a touch of irony. "My people seem not to think much about right and wrong, other than what is right is what is right for Klingons and what is wrong for them is wrong. They veil in ritual their wish not to think about any other rights or wrongs."

As he spoke he paced the office, paused at the far end, then paced to the star-scattered viewport.

"But I was not raised that way," he said. "Right and wrong are matters of thought, not of the fist."

At his desk, Sisko smiled again. "If you're looking for somebody to argue with you, I'm not it. Although I've got a raw knuckle or two of my own. . . ."

Nodding, Worf understood what Sisko meant, that he was tolerantly listening to the troubles of a subordinate, but there seemed to be more here. Worf had things in common with Sisko. They were both big men, and certain physical challenges always came to big men. They were both removed from the cores of their home societies, Worf raised in another star system, then out for years on a starship, Sisko out here on this remote station, trying to keep steady a constantly rocking bowl.

"Whenever I have met Klingons in my life," Worf said, "they have insisted that I must come back to the Klingon fold, or I will pay in the end. But why? Why *must* I be only with my people?"

"I don't believe that's true," Sisko said. "There's more to existence than genetics. You have nothing moral in common with those Klingons out there. So how will you fit?"

Hard words.

Worf looked at him. Sisko was giving him no quarter with those assumptions.

A rough sigh caused a circle of Worf's warm breath to form on the viewport, blotting out the stars. "Then I am lost. . . ."

Ben Sisko pressed his lips flat and got up from his desk chair. He came slowly around the desk, and crossed to the viewport where Worf was gazing rather pointlessly at the stars. He paused and looked out there also.

"There's a thinking process, Mr. Worf, a pattern of sense that every intelligent culture has to develop in order to survive. Eventually any advanced race *must* realize that two plus two equals four, even among Klingons. You have to decide what's more important to you . . . thought, or genetics."

Confused, Worf felt his brow draw tight. "But that is my point. There may not be a choice, sir."

"There's always a choice. We all overcome our genetics in some way or other." Doggedly Sisko cocked his head. "I understand the human couple who adopted you tried to raise you in some semblance of Klingon ways. Is that right?"

"They . . . tried."

"Well, I think they made a mistake. What's it given you but a struggle? It was a disservice to you as an individual to try to make you part of a group you just weren't part of."

Worf stared at him. Never in his life had he heard anything like that statement. As a child he had been teased, of course, but children tease. As an adult, he had been given only approving nods when people heard that his parents had tried to raise him in what they thought was the Klingon way. Now he was hearing something wildly else.

"Klingons can't *always* have been warriors," Sisko went on without apology for what he had said about Worf's parents. "A warrior mentality is a luxury of success. The fighting habit can't be instinct, or there wouldn't be Klingons. You'd have all killed each other a long time ago, or just died out because nobody bothered to grow food or build shelter. A martial culture that desires more than anything to live and die in battle is just not going to survive. Somebody has to deal with the mundane. Somebody has to grow food, somebody has to make clothing—if your whole culture's fighting, you'd better be able to steal those things from someone else. If you can't do that, you die. If you run up on a group of tough farmers and weavers, you die. Like the Vikings of old Earth . . . to them, the only way to make it to Valhalla in the next life was to die in battle. So they could only survive as long as they could steal from others. Eventually, the others just started saying no, and figured out ways to outsmart the power of raw strength. In case you hadn't noticed, the Vikings didn't make it into modern civilization."

"Technology," Worf murmured hoarsely. Shame brought heat to his cheeks. "That is what you are talking about. The Klingons did not develop spacefaring. We stole it from others who landed on our planet. Then we came out into the galaxy . . . and stole more."

Folding his arms and leaning against the viewport's rim, Sisko shook his head. "Your ancestors, Mr. Worf. Somebody else. Complete strangers. Not you. That's my point."

Worf turned away from the window now, shored himself up, and met the other man's eyes. "Thank you, sir."

"You're welcome. Now come back here and sit down. I have something I want to ask you." He pushed off the viewport and strode back around his desk.

Somewhat numb, Worf followed him. "Yes, sir."

When they were both seated, in a way a personal example of the civilized mannerisms Sisko had spoken about, the captain leaned his elbows on his desk and folded his hands again.

"Now tell me," he began, curving the subject gently, "do you have any idea why Gowron would come all the way here just for you?"

Surprised by the question, Worf frowned and mentally shrugged. "Friendship, sir."

"I don't mean to insult you, but I don't know if I

believe that. I find that rather a paper excuse for the highest official of a warring culture venturing into unfriendly territory. So if I don't believe that, then there must be something else. What is it about you, Mr. Worf, that made Gowron take such a chance?"

Baffled, Worf found his mouth hanging open.

"Why," Sisko went on, "would you personally, particularly, be of value to Gowron? Why would he take such a risk to put you on his side in the middle of all this? I suspect he has an underlying motive. Maybe Kira was right. Maybe Gowron doesn't expect the Federation to be around much longer and he wants you on his side to give him information that will make the fall easier."

Stunned, Worf felt his eyes grow tight and his breathing shallow. "I . . . cannot answer such a question, sir. I do not have the answer."

"I didn't think you did. But I'll bet there is one, and I'm going to find out what it is. I'm sorry, Mr. Worf," Sisko said, "but I can't accept your resignation at this time."

He might as well have leaped from his place, charged the room, and plunged a raw fist down Worf's throat. Worf stared, for he had assumed Sisko would be glad to be rid of him.

"I don't understand. . . . What further use could I be here?"

"I'm not sure yet. But as long as the fighting continues between the Klingons and the Cardassians, I need you here on this station."

In the years before this, the time of his service in Starfleet, there had always been a choice. That choice had plagued him day and night. Was he to rise above the gut instinct that made him violent and take anchorage in intellect, or give up all that he had been so graciously given by his adoptive parents and adoptive culture and surrender in to those raging drives? He had always possessed the choice, until this moment.

Now, before him, Benjamin Sisko was evicting the choice. Worf was needed. He would stay.

"If you think that is wise," he uttered, again suggesting that he could be as much liability as aid.

"I don't know if it's wise or not," Sisko said assertively. "But I do know you're a good officer and right now I can use every good officer I can get."

Abruptly deprived of his self-immolation, Worf continued to stare as if two weapons had been wrenched from his fists. It seemed he would fight after all, and the side on which he would fight had also been decided for him. He didn't know whether he was relieved or not.

He parted his lips to say something, but it was also snatched away as Kira Nerys entered the office without announcement. Her heart-shaped face was flushed with excitement, the kind of bulldog flintiness that comes to soldiers only during a war. "Captain, we just got word from Bajoran intelligence that the Klingons have routed the Cardassian fleet."

Sisko didn't seem surprised. "How long until they reach Cardassia Prime?"

"Fifty-two hours."

Worf forced his voice up. "If the Klingon Empire has reverted to its old practices, they will occupy the Cardassian homeworld, execute all government officials, and install an imperial overseer to put down any further resistance."

The captain's black eyes turned hard as rock. The outcome was unacceptable.

"I think it's time to talk to the Cardassians."

"Captain, I'm a little busy at the moment, so whatever you have to say, make it brief."

"Dukat? I was trying to reach someone in the new civilian government."

Gul Dukat. A pompous, sanctimonious example of the sons of Cardassia. There were many like him. As proud as he was of himself, he was nothing unique.

Had he not been so nervous, his pomposity would have served better. For now, it was only a thin veil against the worry that kept sliding through in his face and voice as he spoke to Ben Sisko on the office monitor. Dukat was scared.

"And you succeeded," the Cardassian said. *"You're speaking to the new chief military advisor to the Detepa Council."*

"Does that mean you've turned your back on the Central Command?" Sisko asked.

"It means that as a loyal officer of the Cardassian military, I'm pledged to serve the legitimate ruling body of the Empire. Whoever that may be."

He hated it. The strain of his position came across clearly even through the tiny monitor.

"In other words," Captain Sisko measured, "you saw which way the wind was blowing and switched sides."

"It seemed like a good idea at the time."

Once Dukat had been embarrassed enough for the moment, Sisko shifted attitude.

"You've got to get those council members to safety, Dukat," he said, "before the Klingons reach Cardassia."

Dukat's manner changed very slightly—enough to show that he might actually be relieved to find someone willing to cross channels in his favor and for the sake of those who were being flagrantly attacked.

"I'm open to suggestions."

"If you can get a ship," Sisko instructed, "meet me at . . . these coordinates." He punched a set of numbers into his keypad. "I'll do what I can to escort you out of the war zone."

Dukat's attitude also changed yet again—not only was Sisko willing to warn him, but willing to risk his life, his crew, his own ship in order to help. No one could go untouched from that kind of sacrifice when it was so uncalled for.

"That's a very generous offer, Captain," the Cardassian said without the salt of irony in his voice that had been there a moment ago. *"I must say, I'm touched. By saving the members of the Detepa Council, you'll be saving—"*

"Forget the speech, Dukat. Just meet me at the rendezvous."

"And if the Klingons try to stop us?"

"Then I'll be there to reason with them. I doubt the Klingons will fire on a Federation ship."

"I'm not sure I share your optimism. But then, I don't have much of a choice, do I? We'll meet you there."

From the place where he had stood aside, out of the

scope of the return-feed camera, Worf, still Lieutenant Commander, Starfleet, looked now at Ben Sisko
and understood what Dukat must reluctantly be feeling. Relief, and certainly gratitude for having the
choice made.

Yet there was the prickling doubt that had remained without voice until now, the knowledge that
his own people were not easily frightened, and had
avoided conflict with Starfleet until now.

As Sisko turned to him, Worf said, "Sir, if the
Klingons are right . . . if the Cardassian government
has been taken over by the Founders . . ."

"Then we'll be helping them escape," Sisko finished
for him. "That's a chance we'll have to take. Report to
the *Defiant*, Commander. I know you want to get out
of that uniform, but right now I need you with me."

A ship. Not a starship, not a merchant ship—a war-
ready battleship. And all the time it had been right
here, without his giving it a single thought.

Energy pulsed through his veins and his great heart
pounded. He had a ship again!

CHAPTER
16

Aʜ, ᴛʜɪs ᴏʟᴅ corridor. So many decades, so many changes.

Now a new change, and in the midst of it, yet another new change. Revolution, and now war.

Evacuate the council. Relatively simple.

And the corridor still smelled. Something about the original design of the plumbing. After the first half century, no one wanted to fix the smell, because it had become part of the mystique of the place.

Dukat strolled here with more ease than he had expected. After all, his faction was no longer in power, yet somehow he had survived and been given a new title. He didn't really understand why, but this was not one of those things a soldier questions. Civilian though the new council was, they still had to have a military, and though the new government had purged the military leaders, somehow Dukat was still here.

He would continue doing his job as best he saw it until someone decided to purge him also.

Pausing at the council chamber door, he glanced behind him at his aide and said, "Back me up, Yelu. The ship is ready. All we have to do is clear immediate space and we should be able to rendezvous with Sisko in relative safety. You'll have to hurry these elites along. They're not soldiers. No discipline, you know."

"I understand, Gul Dukat," Yelu said.

Without knocking, Dukat opened the old-fashioned chamber door and strode in.

Under the high ceiling of the ancient council chamber, with its walls draped in tattered but traditional tapestries, the members of the new Detepa Council looked up and were startled at the interruption of their bureaucrating.

There were eleven of them. Dukat knew most of their names, but that wasn't significant. As Yelu took position behind him, Dukat stationed himself somewhere near the middle of the long conference table.

"Councilmen, forgive me for having to interrupt your business day, but there has been a surprise attack."

"An attack?" one of the councilmen blurted. "Where? Here in the capital?"

"No, in space."

"When?"

"Only minutes ago. At the moment, we're not doing very well. There is a significant battle going on near the outer colonies."

"Who would have the nerve to attack us?" another councilman said.

Dukat patiently turned and gave the answer directly to the person who had asked it.

"A Klingon task force has invaded our space and is trying to get here to capture the planet. There is a chance that our ships may hold them off, but I must tell you that in the fervor of revolution you did happen to kill several of our best military commanders, whom you really should have left alive. Our forces, therefore, are strong in numbers, but weak in strategic ability and experience. As such, I am going to evacuate you from the planet and take you to a place of safety."

The councilmen were notably stunned, and they looked at each other in mute question, until finally one of them uttered, "Us?"

Meager, but enough to cause Dukat to continue talking.

"Yes, of course," he said. "As the governing council, you will be the Klingons' first targets. You will need a strong sanctuary. I have a ship waiting to take you into Federation jurisdiction, where you will stay until our home space can be stabilized. Gentlemen, we have to get you out."

They stopped looking at each other, and started gaping at him instead.

Then, sitting Chief Councilman Ewai spoke from his place at the head of the table.

"Have you been drinking, Dukat?"

Dukat's brow furrowed. "I beg your pardon?"

Ewai didn't stand up, but simply frowned and

narrowed his eyes at him. "I have heard nothing of this Klingon invasion force. It's very silent, if it's happening."

"It's happening in space," Dukat said measuredly. "Sound, Councilman, does not travel through the vacuum of space."

Catching the insult squarely, Ewai glanced at a few of the others, then looked back at Dukat. "This is very strange . . . most curious, in fact. Wouldn't this be a perfect way for you and your people to get back in charge? You're going to rescue us, you take us away, and we simply disappear."

Taken aback, Dukat opened his mouth to speak, but for a moment was too astounded by such a suggestion to say anything. He paused, glanced at Yelu, who also appeared to have been cuffed, and finally turned to Ewai.

"You're right," he said. "It would be perfect. Unfortunately, I didn't think of it. Handing the government back to those who have lost it once is simply not my plan."

Councilman Mera spoke up. "I don't believe him. He's part of the old order. I knew we should have done away with any vestige of them when we had the chance! Now the soldiers will follow him instead of us!"

"The soldiers," Dukat derided, "are out there, dying for you in space, trying to protect the homeworld! But at the moment, we don't think we can do it sufficiently. We need more time to stabilize our strength. In the meantime, I have no intention of letting Klingons capture the government of Cardassia.

This way, even if Klingons take the homeworld, they still will not have *us*. I came here to keep the legitimate government out of their hands. Though I shiver to admit it, that legitimate government at the moment is you gentlemen."

"You're hanging yourself, Dukat," Councilman Pelor threatened, but without a threatening tone. He seemed nervous, not used to his own power yet.

"Fine," Dukat said. "The Federation is going to meet us and escort us out of our space. We'll have to set you up as a government in exile. That way, our people will have something to cling to, something to fight for. Certainly you, as revolutionaries, can understand that."

"Wait!" Councilman Gruner stood up sharply, his rounded stomach creating a platform from which his meeting robes hung. "We've been threatening and harassing the Federation for a decade, and they are coming to help us?"

Dukat shrugged. "I don't understand it myself, but that's the way they are."

The table erupted into bellows of argument and disbelief, disagreement and tension, until finally Ewai smashed his palm on the table four or five times and caused the others to fall quiet again.

When they did, he looked again at Dukat with that same glare of unveiled suspicion.

"So you, the weakened and recently overpowered military, just made a deal with the Federation, people we've been trying to wipe out for years, to protect the new council, whom the military hates. I see."

"You do *not* see!" Dukat bellowed, roiled with

frustration at this turn. He genuinely had not expected this, but he couldn't help but comprehend some of it. If he were these people, he probably wouldn't believe himself.

"I agree with Ewai," one of the councilmen said. His name completely faded from Dukat's mind, but it didn't matter. "This would be a perfect way for Dukat and his lackeys to slip back into power!"

"Yes, it would be perfect," Dukat coached. "But that's not what I'm doing. If it were, I would've used this weapon on you already. The Klingons are light-years closer in the time you have been resisting me, and I strongly suggest you get up out of those chairs before you find yourselves dead in them with Klingon blades embedded in your chests. Gentlemen, the doorway is over here—"

"Wait, wait," Councilman Pelor urged, holding his hands out in a complacent manner. "There must be some other way to confirm this."

"We don't have *time* to confirm it!" Yelu called out from behind Dukat.

They all looked at him briefly, then Dukat said, "He's quite correct. No time."

Councilman Mera ignored them. "Who could we get confirmation from, other than the military?"

"How do we even know there's a war going on out there?" Councilman Ewai persisted. "Because Dukat has told us?" He looked up at Dukat. "You could tell us there was a gigantic blue monster in orbit. None of us have any evidence whatever of a force massing on our borders. There hasn't been a single trader come in with that rumor."

"There hasn't been a single trader come in because no one has been able to get through." Dukat canted forward slightly as if scolding a child.

Councilman Locan spoke for the first time, saying, "Perhaps we could send someone out to view this war."

Dukat swung full about and glared at him. "There . . . isn't . . . *time.*"

He had expected some resistance, but not this. After all, he himself had not been purged, so someone in this room must have been impressed enough with his record to trust him. Where was that trust now?

Did they want him to sit behind a desk and move the military about like toys on a model board?

Had they expected only that from him?

Civilians.

Ewai was gazing at him with unbridled suspicion when he turned back again.

"This could all be a grand charade," the chief councilman said. "A ruse to get us all into space on one ship. To scare us right off the planet, where we can be killed."

"The council disappears," Gruner added, "and the old guard walks into power."

"You killed the old guard!" Dukat scorned. "And I, quite honestly, do not want the job!"

Startled briefly by his outburst, the council fell silent again and gawked at him and each other.

After a moment, Pelor made another attempt. "Perhaps you could tell us . . . where you appropriated this information of an impending invasion by the Klingons?"

"I . . . had a source. Because he informed me of what was planned, I was able to prepare a ship in case a quick escape might turn out to be prudent."

"Tell us who your informant is."

"Well . . ."

"Tell us, Dukat," Ewai said, "or we stay here."

"Well, it . . ."

From behind Dukat, squeezed by the tension and anxiety of the moment, Yelu blurted, "It was Garak!"

Dukat squeezed one eye shut, and with the other glowered at his aide and the incredible size of the young soldier's mouth.

"Garak!" Ewai bawled.

"Garak?"

"Garak . . ."

"Garak."

As the name traveled the council chamber, Dukat felt himself becoming more and more shriveled and pointless with every syllable. He made a note to remind himself to have Yelu's tongue cut out as soon as the war was over.

"Yes," he submitted finally, "the first warning came from Garak. Yes, yes, yes. However, within the past hour I received a communiqué from Captain Sisko at *Deep Space Nine,* who informed me that the Klingon task force—"

"Garak . . ." Gruner impugned. "And Sisko."

"Gentlemen, *please . . .*"

"Go away, Dukat," Ewai said scornfully. "Save yourself while you can."

"Councilmen," Dukat persisted, "you must come with me."

"Yes," Pelor taunted. "We come with you, you declare martial law, drive away all contestants, and tell the people you have saved the planet from the Klingons. Once you're back in power, no one will ask what happened to us. I am not going."

"Nor am I."

"Nor I."

"Locan, call the guards."

Dukat leaned to Yelu. "Call *my* guards."

Ewai spoke louder. "If you're going to take us off the planet and kill us, then why should we leave? Don't inconvenience either of us, Dukat."

"Fine!" As Yelu touched the comm unit on his wrist, Dukat drew his disruptor and leveled it squarely at Ewai's face.

The councilmen indulged in a collective gasp as Dukat moved closer and took Ewai by the arm. By now, Yelu had his own rifle poised over the chamber.

"All right, this is enough," Dukat proclaimed. "True, I am not thrilled with you. But this government is going to survive if I have to kill you and stuff you and set you up on some planet as the legitimate, recognized government of Cardassia. You fought to be the heads of the government and that's what you're going to be. It's all yours now. When history is written, you were in charge when everything fell apart. And you're coming along to watch it all happen. The door is over *there!*"

Yelu pressed his cheek to the butt of his rifle and swung to cover them as the councilmen stared in shock. At the other end of the room Dukat kept the more ornery of those in the chamber in line until pounding footsteps in the old corridor signaled the approach of one set of guards or the other.

Would they be the council house guards? Or would they be Dukat's soldiers?

Hearing that sound, Councilman Ewai refused to move until he knew for sure that he had no choice.

The chamber was eerily silent, but for the tense breathing of the thirteen beings there.

The footsteps pounded nearer.

Dukat waited with rather less of a thumping heart than he had expected. He had waited for days upon days to be called before the council, questioned, and ultimately executed, but that had not happened, no matter how he prepared himself for it.

Yet, relief did wash through him as uniformed soldiers poured in the narrow, tall doorway and flocked along the oldest tapestry, their weapons shouldered because they had not yet been told at whom to aim.

"Now, Councilmen," Dukat announced when the shuffling and rushing settled down to a tense stillness, "I'm going to save you if I have to do it over your dead bodies. Yelu, you take one rank and go first. Weapons on full. Second rank, set your weapons on stun and aim them at the councilmen. If any fails to come with us, shoot him down and carry him to the ship. Councilmen, the door."

With one rank thumping in front, the councilmen shuffling in the center, and a second rank of soldiers thumping behind, Dukat put his own disruptor to Ewai's throat and pressed him forward.

The old halls had never seemed so large, so long,

and so very imposing. Of course, he had never had to escape from them before.

Odd! With all that was going on in the open galaxy, here he was, escaping from Cardassia Prime!

The council guards had been summoned, and met them in the courtyard—weapons flaring.

"Return fire!" Yelu's voice carried rather well on the flat stone court.

So did the whine of weapons fire.

Dukat saw three of his soldiers go down, and four guards, in the opening round of crossfire.

"Keep them occupied," he ordered the nearest guard, then waved his disruptor and with that gesture herded the councilmen around the back of the huge old hall to the private launch area.

Anxious not to be caught in the snap and whine of crossfire, the councilmen ducked their heads and ran as they were bade.

"Into the ship!" Dukat called. "Quickly!"

Whether they accepted him at his word now that they actually saw that there was a ship and not a hanging post in this yard, Dukat could not tell and did not care. He pushed the last of them inside, then motioned his soldiers to go back and support the others. They had orders to break off and disperse as soon as the ship launched, so he would be doing them a favor by launching as quickly as he could manage.

Inside the stout and serviceable ship was a skeleton crew of six. Dukat would pilot. He simply didn't trust anyone else.

"Gentlemen, all of you sit quietly and do not attempt any movements which my crew will consider dangerous to me or to the vessel. We are taking you away from here. Indulge in your fantasies and your fears. The truth will find you soon enough."

Sliding into the pilot's cubicle, he fired up the antigravs. A roar of power came up under the vessel. The ground peeled away beneath them. A moment later, the city.

He felt the eyes of the captive councilmen as he engaged thrusters and flew the ship into the thin atmosphere and out into the blackness of space. Through large viewing ports on either side of the transport cabin, the planet fell away and space swelled up. Service lights came on in the cabin, very dim, just enough to move without tripping.

As soon as he could, Dukat increased speed to full impulse and steered impatiently around the outer planets. This was not a particularly powerful vessel, but it was double-hulled and possessed enough weapons to allow for a few good defensive hits.

His heart was pounding in his chest. Imagine that. He had actually been excited by stealing the council!

Yes, it was invigorating to rescue these one-dimensional civilians. He, the military, had just rescued the civilian council put in power when they deposed the military council.

Life was twisted.

Keying his sensors to automatic, he boosted the ship to warp speed, then warp two, and warp three. That was its highest speed. If they encountered ships that were faster, they would have to fight. He set his mind to that, but planned more sensibly to make a clean escape without any such incidents.

He knew the chances of clean escape were endangered. When the Klingon force found themselves met by the Cardassian fleet, they would know they had been found out, and Dukat estimated their next step, if they could free a ship or two, would be to block any escape from this sector. Time would tell.

He felt the eyes of Ewai, Pelor, Gruner, Locan, and all the others. They expected to be gunned down unceremoniously. Why not? They had done that to those whose power they had wrested away.

Such was the way of governments. Dukat had seen it before.

The sensors jolted him out of his contemplations when, after only fifteen minutes in space, they began bleeping loudly and showing flashing lights on his pilot panel.

"Contact," he said to his navigator. "I was afraid of this. I hope Sisko hurries."

"There they are!" the navigator called, and pointed out one of the side windows.

Ewai bolted to his feet and glared out the window. "Those are Klingons!"

"Yes!" Dukat shouted. "Those are Klingons! Unless you think I stole Birds-of-Prey and I'm having them attack us for effect! You must think I am quite a showman."

Stunned, Ewai sank back into his seat, staring out the window.

"How many?" Dukat asked his navigator.

"I read three . . . perhaps four coming out of cloak. They are at a notable distance. Shall I try to outmaneuver them?"

"Yes, try. We're smaller. We can take tighter turns. Shields up . . . go to emergency defensive posture. All we have to do is gain time until Sisko gets here. I hope he gets here soon."

"Make sure the chief double-checks all the new systems. We may need them."

"I'll tell him. But knowing the chief, he's probably doing it already."

Sisko modified his step enough for Kira to keep up as he hurried along the curve of the docking ring.

"Keep the station on yellow alert," he went on, skimming the top of the hundred thoughts rushing through his head. He was about to divide himself— captain of a fighting ship, custodian of a critical outpost, and he just couldn't be in two places at the same time. "I'd recommend moving some of the civilian population down to Bajor."

"I was planning to," she said, in a way that let him know they were thinking alike, and that in his absence she would defend *Deep Space Nine* with all the vigorous commitment of her years as an underground fighter, protecting the station and its reasons for being here as heartily as she had once fought for her planet, for her own life, and during the worst times for a simple meal.

In a very real way, she was still fighting for the planet and her life, for if the Klingons took Cardassia, they would come here next, to the wormhole, and Bajor.

"I still wish I were going with you," she said.

Sisko could tell she wasn't really asking to go. She knew how much she would be needed here if things turned sour.

"So do I," he gave her in return. "Take care of the place while I'm gone."

She nodded. Simple words, simple trust. All they could do was their jobs as best they and their crews could manage. The outcome—who could tell?

Without dragging out the goodbyes, Kira nodded and hurried away. Abruptly Sisko felt bad at leaving her with the heavy end of the stick, but the idea of sending her out to do his job against the Klingons, on what was quickly becoming a battlefront, was even worse.

"Ben! Ben!"

Echoes? Couldn't be—

He turned. Yes, it was. Kasidy Yates was rushing toward him down the corridor.

"I'm glad I caught you before you left!" She came up close.

"So am I," he said. But he wasn't. Another brutal goodbye—didn't sit well. "When did you get in?"

"Less than an hour ago. Jake told me you were about to go off on some kind of mission."

Her chocolate eyes belied the truth—she knew what the mission was, or at least she sensed it. She had been part of the beginning.

"The *Defiant* leaves in a few minutes," he said, and in many ways that was his answer. Not a runabout, not a transport, but the *Defiant*.

"And you can't tell me about it," she allowed.

He tried to smile. "I'll be back in four or five days."

"I'm leaving tomorrow," she said, disappointment filling her eyes and bracketing her mouth.

"I guess," Sisko sighed, "our timing hasn't been too good."

"It's been terrible." Kasidy's face was a template of regrets, of secret loneliness, and now of crumbled hopes. Even in peacetime, it was a very big galaxy. "I'm not even sure when I'll be back."

"Make it soon," he said to her, knowing as well as she did that the vagaries of commerce, not the two of them, would decide when they saw each other again.

She gazed at him, her throat moving as she struggled for words, but no farewell would serve and they both knew it.

Ultimately she flew forward and they pressed into a kiss, struggling to make up for the time lost, time spent together when they were busy telling themselves they just weren't "ready," whatever that meant.

All at once it didn't mean much at all, and they had lost a very great deal.

"Don't get killed," she murmured against his ear.

Knowing lost time couldn't be retrieved, Sisko set her back an inch or two.

"I'll do my best."

She let him go without any more pain. In fact, she turned and walked away before he entered the airlock leading to the *Defiant.*

Stepping onto the bridge of the *Defiant* was like putting his feet into an ice-cold bath. He had no sensations of progress or allurement that usually struck him when he was about to take the ship out. This time there could only be resolution. This was no skirmish. This was real war.

Maybe the bridge really was too cool. He thought about asking somebody to warm it up a little, but changed his mind. Adrenaline would take over and he'd be plenty warm enough.

Bashir was here, and Dax at the helm, Worf at the sensors and communications, and Ensign Helen Blake at the weapons and tactical. He didn't know her very well and this wasn't the time for a cocktail party. At other stations were other officers whom he acknowledged with little glances as he took his command seat.

"Sisko to Ops," he said, keying his comm pad.

"Kira here."

"Release all docking clamps and restrain all other traffic until we get under way."

"Aye-aye . . . Clamps are off. The pylon is free of traffic. You're clear to launch, sir. Good luck."

"Thank you, Major. Take care of my station."

"Aye, sir. Take care of my border."

He imagined her tense smile, and it gave him sustenance. The Klingons might stir up ghastly trouble, but they weren't going to have it their own way. They were giving in to primitive fears, lashing out at anything in sight, and for that they would have to pay some price.

It would be for Sisko to dictate that price.

As the *Defiant* slid away from *Deep Space Nine* and launched into open space, he settled into the leather of his chair.

"Activate cloaking device," he said right off.

Blake complied. The lights dimmed as if the ship were a living thing ducking into trouble.

"Cloaking device is functioning within normal parameters," she reported. She was tense.

Sisko didn't blame her. "Dax, set a course for the rendezvous point. Maximum warp."

Dax glanced down at her controls, tapped in the

required instructions to the ship's mainframe, then said, "Course laid in."

"Engage. Mr. Worf, keep an eye out for Klingon vessels, cloaked or otherwise."

"Aye, sir," the heavy voice rumbled.

A little uneasy, Sisko noted. "Something wrong, Mr. Worf?"

"No, sir. It's just . . . I've never been on a Federation ship that had a cloaking device," Worf admitted. "It's a little strange."

"You'll get used to it."

"Sir," Bashir said hesitantly, "I hate to bring this up, but our agreement with the Romulans expressly prohibits the use of the cloaking device in the Alpha Quadrant."

A stab of irritation ran up Sisko's spine. If he hated to bring it up, why did he? Especially when he knew that his commanding officer knew it perfectly well? He almost snapped something back about instructive comments made to superiors, but that was no way to start a mission that might never end in their lifetimes.

"You're right, it does," he said. "But there are several hundred Klingon ships between us and Dukat, and I intend to make that rendezvous in one piece."

Bashir squeezed up a smile. He didn't seem to realize he'd overstepped his place. "Well, I won't tell the Romulans if you don't."

Open space was shocking in its vastness. To have a perception of the speed—warp eight—was to understand how eternally empty space really was. The time it took to cross what was now a frontier was daunting to the mind that could conceive of the speed they were traveling. With each light-year, they became more and more alone out here, more reliant upon their own wills and resourcefulness, and that much more likely not to make it back alive.

Space was particularly black, with few stars in this sector and almost no other life than on Bajor, way back there, a factor that had made Bajor easy for the Cardassians to occupy for so many years. No one else had wanted it. No one but the Bajorans.

The Federation's here now, he thought, projecting his own will forward to those whom today he would try to protect. Cardassians, if that could be believed. How things could change.

"Captain," Worf said, shaking Sisko out of his thoughts. "I'm detecting some debris, bearing zero-two-five mark three-one-nine."

Without meaning to, he lowered his voice, almost as though he meant to whisper, to keep his identity under wraps and their approach secret. "Commander, drop to one-quarter impulse."

"Aye, Captain," Dax responded.

Worf peered into his readout screens. "It appears to be wreckage from a number of Cardassian vessels."

Sisko tilted forward. "On screen."

The main view shifted, drawing through its powerful sensors and computer-generated magnifications a view of three spade-shaped Galor-class warships.

They were shattered. Hulls relatively intact, but obviously compromised and fully adrift. No power emanations at all, no operating motive power.

"Any sign of survivors?" Bashir automatically asked.

For several seconds, no one answered, as if no one wanted to state the initial reactions.

Then Dax said, "I suppose it's possible, but there's no way to know without decloaking and using our primary sensor array."

Worf turned to Sisko. "Sir, I strongly recommend against deactivating our cloak." When the rest of the crew looked at him as if he were some kind of black-hooded executioner, he said, "It is likely there are cloaked Klingon warships in the vicinity lying in wait."

Bashir boldly turned to him. "Doesn't sound very honorable to me."

Fielding the bald insult, Worf scowled. "In war, nothing is more honorable than victory."

They all watched him; then one by one the glances turned to Sisko and waited for what he would say. Abruptly he was the one who felt like an executioner.

Maybe they all were. Run and hide, or turn and kill.

But there were times to kill, just as there were times to do everything else. The Cardassians had played their part in this. If they had been a more open society, participating in the free exchange of trade and ideas, maybe they wouldn't fall under such easy suspicion, even from suspicious types.

"Commander," he said to Dax, "keep us at one-quarter impulse until we clear the wreckage, then take us to warp."

Bashir was ready. "Sir, if there *are* survivors—"

"I'm sorry, Doctor, but we can't risk it. We have to reach Dukat."

Reluctantly accepting the grim color of the next few days—if only it could be just days—Bashir backed off and didn't press the ugly point, the only point it was really his job to press.

Feeling as if he'd been hollowed out, Sisko pushed out of his command chair. "I'll be in Engineering. I want to check those power grids. We have to be ready for anything. Under these circumstances, we don't know who'll turn on us."

"Aye, sir," Dax murmured. Evidently she wasn't unaffected by the plying guilt in Bashir's voice a moment ago.

The engineering deck on *Defiant* was a maze of power packs. Almost everything down here was geared for engine thrust, maneuvering thrust, and weapons force. On the bridge, everything seemed relatively even, but down here, systems like sensor integrity, environmental control, even life support, were shunted out of the main area. Here, in the putty-and-fog grays of Engineering, the only consideration was strength, and slightly behind that, survival by brutality. This was a kicking ship, and nowhere was that more evident than in its bowels.

Bashir's request was still echoing in Sisko's head. Since coming to DS9 he hadn't had to flatly abandon anyone, not without a fight. But if he strayed from every mission under these conditions, he would find himself sacrificing hundreds for twos and threes, and better not to get in that habit. Things were different.

He snapped at the engineers and made them run down the systems with him, as much to distract himself from the echo of Bashir's words and the picture in his mind of those Galor-class ships drifting pathetically through empty space, out here where no one else would happen on them.

Finally he found a problem and plunged into it, communicating his dissatisfaction with the slightest glitch. If he had to pass by possible survivors, then he was at least going to succeed in saving those he was out here to save.

"And double-check the secondary power grid. It's still not performing as well as it should."

He was instructing one of the engineers when he realized there was another presence standing beside him.

The engineer glanced up, then nodded and quickly vanished.

Above Sisko as he crouched beside the grid housing, Worf glared down at him. "Can I speak with you a moment?"

Sisko stood up. "What can I do for you, Mr. Worf?"

"Sir, I wanted to know . . . why did you assign me to communications instead of tactical?"

Running over a half-dozen possible answers, Sisko decided on the truth—since they were on their way to do the very thing he had tried to avoid for Worf.

"I didn't want to put you in the position of having to fight your own people," he said.

Worf might have realized that.

Sisko couldn't tell.

"I see," the Klingon said.

Sisko shifted. "If you'd like, I could put you in charge of one of the damage-control teams. That way, if there's trouble, you won't have to be on the bridge at all."

Judging from Worf's expression, the concept had never occurred to him, and the offer made him look as if he'd tasted something stale.

"If it's all the same to you, sir, I would prefer to remain on the bridge."

Sisko nodded. "I was hoping you'd say that. As far as I'm concerned, that's where you belong." He paused a moment, then decided to push. "I've been giving your resignation some thought."

Going a little stiff, Worf drew a breath and held it as if expecting to get punched in the face. He pressed his lips tight and waited to hear what Sisko would say.

Taking that as a sign that he was right to butt in, Sisko said, "If you really want to quit Starfleet, I won't stand in your way. I'll approve your request as soon as we get back to the station."

With his words, he talked of resigning. With his eyes and his tone, he let slip the fact the he thought this kind of action would be a fabulous mistake and a waste on two fronts. Not only would Starfleet lose, but Worf would. Many misfits had found substance within the braids of Starfleet service, vaulting far beyond the expectations of any of those childhood teasings that so often prickled men with pasts like Worf's. He not only belonged here—he had flourished here.

Unable to see Worf behind the helm of some distant cargo barge on a thready trade route that lasted years at a time, Sisko waited and kept drilling him with that I'm-pushing-push-back look.

Worf looked unhappy. "I would . . . appreciate that, sir."

As if he'd been slapped, he turned and left the engineering deck.

And that, for Sisko, was worth a smile.

"Have you got the shrapnel-nosed tubes ready yet?"

"Been ready for nearly a month."

"What about the automatic aiming sensors? I don't think we should have to aim by hand all the time."

"They can be keyed with one touch. On, off, just like that. Nothing to it. And here are the light-seekers . . . and right over here the heavy-duty close-range salvos. You know, I never thought I'd be saying this, but right now I'm glad the Dominion's around. Otherwise we never would've started these upgrades, let alone have them finished by now."

"There's something to be said for incentive."

Kira Nerys rolled her eyes at O'Brien's words, but she knew what he meant. The Federation hadn't seen fit to spice up the defenses of DS9 until a threat whispered through from the other side of the wormhole. Suddenly they who were until now only a way station became a frontier fort, and that was how they were going to behave.

Beside her at the engineering station in Ops, Miles O'Brien shook his head and uttered, "I sure hope everything works."

She looked at him. "You're saying you're not sure?"

The new systems were stable enough in and of themselves, but until now any concerns had gone unvoiced about whether or not they would integrate safely into the Cardassian design of the station. There hadn't been time for a complete gutting of the hull and replacement of all parts with Starfleet-coded parts, so O'Brien had been spit-and-pinning things together. Only two of the station's original six fusion reactors had ever worked since Starfleet took over, and since those two provided enough power to run the life-support and general functions of the station, nobody had ever mentioned maybe someday getting into a war and needing more power for strong new weapons.

And there hadn't been time for tests, either.

"The way I see it," he told her finally, "there are two possibilities. Either everything'll be fine . . ."

"Or?"

"Or . . . we'll end up blowing the station to pieces."

She scalded him with a stare. "Let's hope we don't have to find out."

CHAPTER
17

"WHAT'S OUR STATUS?"

Ben Sisko slid into the command chair as Jadzia Dax relinquished it to him. Worf and Bashir were at their stations, neither having much to say to each other, or anyone else, it seemed.

"We're approaching the rendezvous point," Dax told him.

"Sir," Worf said, "I'm detecting signs of weapons fire ahead. There appear to be three Birds-of-Prey attacking a Cardassian vessel. The Cardassian ship is badly damaged."

Dax barely waited for Worf to finish. "Captain, I'm picking up a distress signal from Dukat. Audio only."

"Put him through."

As Dax struggled to pull the crackling signal in, Sisko inched forward in his seat.

The signal was distorted, scratchy.

"This is Gul Dukat of the cruiser Prakesh. *We're under heavy fire. Our shields are failing. I don't know how much longer we can hold out. Send reinforcements immediately. I repeat, this is—"*

"We're in visual range," Dax reported.

Sisko nodded. "On screen. Maximum magnification."

The screen smoothly changed, so smoothly as to suggest a technical loveliness to what it saw.

There before them was a bulky Cardassian ship, dipping uselessly to avoid fire from an incoming Klingon Bird-of-Prey. The bird had its wings down in attack position, its algae-green hull reflecting the light from a small lifeless binary system to their port side.

It came in high and swooped down upon the Cardassian ship, strafing it with a continuous stream of disruptor fire that cut across the Cardassians' deflectors with a scalpel effect, some needles of energy managing to pierce the failing shields and cut into the victim's hull.

"What are your orders, Captain?" Worf's voice shook Sisko out of a nearly hypnotic stare.

Bashir was staring too. They were giving themselves a moment of pause to absorb what they were seeing, the full impact of those disruptors thrumming back to all their home planets.

"Two decades of peace," the doctor said, "and it all comes down to this."

"Benjamin," Dax said quietly, "Dukat's ship's not going to last much longer."

Sisko glowered at the screen. Until now, he'd entertained tiny hopes that something would happen to put this off, that perhaps he could reach Dukat before the Klingons did, and together the Cardassian Council and the Federation could find some way to stay this terrible turn.

Now there was no hope of that. Shots had been fired.

"Arm photon torpedoes," he said. "Drop the cloak and raise the shields. We're going in."

PART
FOUR

CHAPTER
18

"RED ALERT."

As the day lights popped off and were replaced by the eye-saving cranberry lights of alert status, Ben Sisko gripped the arms of his command chair.

Bashir immediately left the bridge, headed for the medical bay, where he would probably be very much needed in a few minutes, and others also hurried after him, on their way to more hands-on positions on the ship's lower decks.

Now the bridge was a tight entity, lightly manned and almost quiet with anticipation.

On the screen before him, molten matter poured from the Cardassian ship as the Klingon Birds-of-Prey tipped up on their wings and veered in for another hit.

He tilted his head toward Worf, but didn't turn.

"Commander, transmit a Priority One signal to the Klingon ship. Tell them to break off their attack and stand down immediately."

Without saying anything, Worf worked his monitor, then turned to Sisko again. "Message sent. Sir, I find it highly unlikely that the Klingons will heed your—"

Sisko wanted to shout a brisk shut-up to him. The message had to be in his alert log, to prove that he gave the Klingons fair warning. Worf must have known that.

Suddenly *Defiant* was hammered with enemy fire. The deck tilted downward, then quickly recovered, leaving them all with a queasy sensation in their stomachs and knees like butter.

"We're been fired upon by the lead Bird-of-Prey. Shields are holding."

"I see what you mean, Mr. Worf," Sisko said with a twinge of sarcasm. "Let's show them what they're up against." He swung to Blake at weapons control. "Attack pattern Omega. Target their engines."

"Aye, Captain."

"And Dax, try to get between them and the Cardassian ship. If we can take those hits on our shields, they may have time to get to a life craft."

"I doubt their life crafts will be operational," Worf reported. "I'm reading exceptionally heavy damage on their ship's underside. Evidently the Klingons have no intention of letting them escape." He looked at Sisko. "It's not the ship the Klingons are after."

Turning up on the edge of her own clamshell form, *Defiant* easily took a tight circle and swept inside the firing parameters of the Klingon vessels, turning loose a volley of heavy phaser fire at the lead bird.

"Got it!" Bashir called out. "You hit their engines!"

Blake nodded. Her face was glossy with sweat.

"They're breaking off," Dax said. "Just the lead ship, though."

Disruptor fire struck them again with the force of a blockhouse kick in the guts. Combative ferocity spilled through them all, and they hunched to their stations.

"Incoming message from the Cardassian ship," Worf reported, his frustration showing in his posture.

"Put it through."

Sisko got up and went to a monitor, where Dukat's face was waiting for him.

"I must compliment you, Captain. You're nearly Cardassian in your punctuality."

In the background, Dax was ordering, "Fire phasers."

Incendiary darts launched from *Defiant* with such force that Sisko had to clutch the edge of the console to keep from stumbling. This ship sure was a power pack.

"Dukat," he said, "power up your engines and prepare to follow us back to DS9."

"An excellent suggestion," the Cardassian said, *"assuming I had any engines left."*

Whoops.

"What's your status?" Sisko asked.

In the background, Dax was choreographing, "Evasive maneuver Gamma Six."

He didn't bother to turn to ask why she was engaging in evasive maneuvers instead of offensive ones. He'd be back in his chair to take over in a minute.

"Our engines are gone," Dukat was saying, *"our shields are down, and we have no weapons to speak of."*

Frustrated, Sisko felt sweat break out on his forehead and neck. All right, they'd do it the hard way.

"Prepare to evacuate. We'll begin beaming you over as soon as possible."

Dukat seemed desperate, but perplexed. *"You'll have to drop your shields to use your transporters."*

"Let me worry about that. Sisko out."

He was jolted back when the ship was hit by a broadax blow. Sparks at tactical—fire on the bridge!

When Sisko regained his balance, Ensign Blake was on the deck, unconscious. Sparks burned her face, but she wasn't awake to notice. She was down for the duration.

He almost started over to tactical himself, but Worf beat him to it, taking the weapons position as if it were a well-worn set of gloves slipping onto his hands.

"Mr. Worf?" Sisko began as he struggled back across the inclined deck to his command center.

"Weapons ready, Captain," Worf said evenly.

As crossfire lashed the *Defiant,* Sisko accepted Worf's position with a nod.

"Sir," Worf said immediately, "restricting our fire to their engines has not proven effective."

Clear enough. Shoot to kill.

That was the recommendation of his new weapons officer. Sisko decided he'd better take it, and realized he'd been doing Worf a disservice by keeping him from firing on their mutual enemy.

"Very well," he said. "Target at your discretion."

Worf responded without a hint of regret. In fact, he seemed relieved. "Aye-aye, Captain."

The phasers were brought up to full power, strong enough to cut a planet apart.

"Pick one of the ships, Dax, and go after it," Sisko said. "Don't try to take them all on at once. There— that one!"

"Aye-aye," Dax said, and leaned into her controls.

The *Defiant* scrolled out of her attack pattern and went one-on-one with the nearest Klingon ship. Both ships unloaded their full power at each other, creasing space with blistering energy, cutting apart asteroids that got in the way and showering each other with the remains.

POOM POOM POOM—the shots echoed as the shields struggled to absorb or bank off all that energy. It was like a bad headache.

Bulldoggishly the *Defiant* plowed after the one Klingon bird, relentlessly refusing to be distracted by the other ships, until finally they came up underneath the bird and opened fire at what was apparently a weak spot in their shields that didn't show up on *Defiant*'s sensors.

Before them, the Klingon ship erupted into a blowtorch, and was vaporized.

"Scratch one Klingon," Sisko said with unveiled admiration. "Was that a lucky shot?"

Worf turned. "Yes, sir. I *was* aiming at their power coils, but I punched through to their warp core."

"I'll take it. Good shooting, Mr. Worf."

"Thank you, sir."

Dax attracted him with a tilt of her head. She was

too busy to actually turn. "Dukat's ship is under fire. I don't know how much longer they can hold out."

"Another Klingon ship has decloaked," Worf reported. "It is a Vor'Cha–class attack cruiser."

Not good. The rush of having taken out one of the Birds-of-Prey was abruptly swallowed by the appearance of this new opponent. Even a power pack like the *Defiant* couldn't manage that many vessels, with one being an attack cruiser. Better to cut and run before they lost everything.

He leaned an elbow hard on his chair's arm. "Sisko to transporter bay. Get ready to start beaming aboard the survivors."

"Aye, Captain," the standing officer replied.

"Sisko to Bashir. Prepare to receive casualties, Doctor. And have security standing by. I want our guests to undergo blood screenings."

"Understood."

Still hammering the enemy ships and doing some real damage, Dax uttered something, but Sisko didn't hear what she said. When he glanced at her, she was still firing full-out volleys at the new wave of Klingon vessels, keeping them from pulling into any good attack formation.

Worf took an instant to look at Sisko and ask, "Blood screenings?"

"Just in case Martok was right."

"Benjamin," Dax interrupted, "it's going to take us at least two minutes to evacuate Dukat's ship. Even with the *Defiant*'s armor, I don't think we can last that long with our shields down."

He was about to respond when Worf spoke up.

"Sir, I have a suggestion."

Sisko looked up at him. He'd been concentrating so much on Worf's personal problems that he had let himself forget that Worf was, in spite of his private torments and questions, an experienced starship bridge officer with years of experience under his belt.

As the lights of phaser attack and heavy hits reflected on their faces, the two men looked at each other.

"Go, Mr. Worf."

"Sir," the Klingon quickly informed him, "it may be possible to modulate this ship's tractor beams to act as additional shields, and push off a portion of the disruptor fire long enough to beam those people aboard."

"Do you know how to do it?"

"I believe I could do it."

"Permission to do so. Pick up any system you need. Dax, free up the tractor system to the tactical station."

She looked dubious, but didn't say anything. Outside, space was a firebox and in moments they might fall into it if they couldn't put off the Vor'Cha cruiser.

It was on their tail, drilling without pause, pumping disruptor fire onto their aft shields. The *Defiant* was standing up to it, but not without shields.

Dax kept up firing, but it was beginning to cost. The ship was whining around them, straining to keep launching deadly energy back at the attackers while also gaining speed after having been hammered so badly. *Defiant*'s power reserves were being channeled into keeping the attackers off the Cardassian transport, always shooting at whatever Klingons were closer to the Cardassian vessel while ignoring the ones closer to *Defiant,* and taking the throttling they could otherwise have fought off. These were agonizing minutes.

"Captain," Worf said a long two minutes later, "I believe it can be done now."

"Are we in transporter range of Dukat's ship?"

"Thirty seconds," Dax said. She watched her board without raising her eyes. "Twenty-five . . . twenty . . ."

"Ready, Mr. Worf."

"Standing by, sir."

"Ten . . ."

"Dax, prepare to drop the shields. Transporter room, this is Sisko. Stand by to transport on my mark."

"Five . . ."

"Mr. Worf, engage the tractor beam. Let's push 'em off."

CHAPTER
19

"IT'S WORKING, BENJAMIN!"

Jadzia Dax raised her eyes to look at the aft
viewscreen, showing a bizarre vision of the attack
ship being choked back by a funnel of diffused tractor
beam. They were still firing, but the disruptor fire was
measurably reduced, and the impacts on the ship
turned from deafening cracks to kettledrum booms.

"You were right, Mr. Worf," she said. "The modu-
lated tractor beam's deflecting some of the Klingon
disruptor fire."

"Disruptors effectiveness at fifty percent," Worf
reported, as if he hadn't had anything to do with it.

"Well done, Mr. Worf," Sisko offered. "Lower
shields. Sisko to transporter bay—begin emergency
transport."

"Transport under way."

The ship rocked violently as if caught in a vise, almost as if its own tractor beam were acting as an anchor. But that was just a feeling.

"The ablative armor is holding," Dax reported.

Another hit chorused Worf's report. "Klingon ships are closing. Armor on the port side is losing integrity."

Sisko leaned to his comm. "Transporter bay, what's our status?"

"Captain, this is Dukat. Almost half the council members are still on my ship. We need at least another minute."

There was a momentary otherworldliness about having Dukat answer his question—about having Dukat participating in a cooperative manner at all, never mind having that voice pump up from the lower decks, at somebody else's station. They must really be busy down there for the transporter chief to let that happen.

"Another minute," Sisko murmured, in his mind enduring a flurry of all the mathematics of how much firepower and how much armament one more minute meant in molecules. Stress points and impact factors, joint pressure reflux and sheet thickness—how much could the ship really absorb?

"Looks like we're going to find out just how much of a pounding this ship can take," he found himself saying aloud. It didn't sound any better than when he had kept it to himself.

"The Klingons have closed in to point-blank range," Worf said loudly, over the throttling of disruptor fire from outside.

On the screen, Klingon ships bore down and mauled the *Defiant* with coordinated strafes, igniting the sky into a bravura of molten matter peeling sheet by sheet from the *Defiant*'s hull.

In firm response the *Defiant* pumped back volley upon volley, smashing into the pursuing ships' forward screens and occasionally blasting through to the hard metal. By the time they reached DS9, a couple of those ships might be beyond practical repair under these condition.

If he had anything to do with it, they would.

Strike upon strike rattled through the *Defiant*'s outer aft shields until one made it through and caused the ship to wobble on its course. He held tight to the command seat as bridge officers around him were thrown from their posts into pools of sparks cast from erupting panels.

"Ablative armor has failed," Dax called over the whine of straining systems. "We've got plasma leaks on decks two, three, and five, and we've lost our aft torpedo launchers."

Without responding to her, Sisko leaned at the comm and spoke clearly over the howling ship. "Doctor?"

"We've got them."

Sisko sat up straight and with a glaze of victory snapped, "Raise shields! Activate the cloak."

Had they heard him? His ears were whining.

"I'm not getting any response from the cloaking device," Dax called. After a moment she apparently thought he hadn't heard her, because she said again, "It's not working."

"That should make the trip home a little more

interesting," Sisko said, by way of calming those around him. "Set a course for DS9, maximum warp."

As the *Defiant* banked hard into warp speed, the departure-angle viewer showed a crackling picture of the Cardassian ship, now hopefully abandoned, as it exploded into an incendiary ball.

The remaining Bird-of-Prey and the attack cruiser turned their sterns on it with panache, and bolted to warp speed, in direct hot pursuit of the *Defiant*.

Julian Bashir had been surrounded by patients in a disaster situation before, but never by Cardassians.

They were everywhere, dozens of them, and he would've been lying to say it didn't twist his stomach a little. No one could have lived so closely with Bajorans for so long without having picked up a little of that baked-in unease about their former slave drivers.

Working to mend their wounds was good therapy, though, and he soon found himself well distracted.

Except when he had to give the blood screening. That was a bit nerve-racking. He knew the chances were slim, far better that the Klingons were overreacting to rumor . . . yet, still, the changelings were a terrifying force in the expanding galaxy, and he himself admitted that he was afraid. For whatever his patients were, Cardassian or changeling, he was glad of the Starfleet security officers at the door.

Because Sisko knew shapeshifters and how elusive they were, security guards were posted in pairs every few yards, and there were phaser rifles set on full power in their hands. The guards were on constant surveillance, looking, guessing, searching, with their rifles pointed in various directions through the area as each of the council members was tested and okayed.

Strange—imagine the Cardassian council being the least threat aboard a Federation ship . . . how times could change.

Least of all was the ever-tormenting acquaintance Gul Dukat, who now stood and said, "Thank you, Doctor. Now, if you don't mind, I'd like to go to the bridge."

Bashir nodded, and turned to him with a blood-sequencing syringe. "This will only take a minute. Your arm, please."

Reminded of the loss of his ship by the unremitting pounding that thrummed through the hull every few seconds, Dukat flared with outrage. Evidently he knew. "What's the meaning of this?"

"Just a simple blood screening."

"I assure you," Dukat said loftily, "I am not a changeling."

"Then you have nothing to worry about."

"I find this whole procedure offensive."

Bashir nodded. Yet another.

"And I find you offensive," he said. "Now hold out your arm or I'll have a security officer do it for you."

Encouraged by another pitch of the deck beneath them and a roar of strain rushing down the bulkheads, Dukat held out his gangly arm.

Bashir buried a sigh—not exactly of relief. That was yet to come, if at all.

"Dukat's on his way up, Benjamin." Jadzia Dax found a moment to cast Sisko a toying glance as she piloted the battleship at blinding speed through the covert folds of space, toward the fortress that would be their survival.

"Just what I always wanted," Sisko cracked. "Two Klingons on my tail and Dukat on my bridge."

"I can't wait to hear him have to thank you for saving him and his council."

Sisko eyed the monitors, giving off numerical readings of the two ships racing after them. "You don't expect that, do you?"

"Oh, I think he'll feel obliged to do it now, rather than have to do it later, possibly in public," she said as she urged the ship up another half point in lightspeed. "But I do think he'll start complaining first."

Sisko shook his head. "Not even Dukat could be quite that ungracious."

"No? I'll make you a bet."

"What kind of bet?"

She turned so that he could see a quarter of her face, enough to show that she was smiling.

"I'll bet you a five-course dinner that he starts complaining within ten seconds of stepping onto the bridge."

"Taken," Sisko said. The unlikely, untimely banter gave him a jolt of hope. "But you'd better be ready for—"

He never got to finish. The turbolift hissed, and Dukat stepped onto the bridge, flanked by a security guard as tall as he was and twice as burly.

"Captain," Dukat said, "would you inform this security guard that he doesn't have to monitor my every move? It makes me feel unwelcome."

Admittedly surprised, Sisko glanced at Dax.

"You owe me a dinner, Benjamin," she said.

Dukat looked at her, then back to Sisko. "What is that supposed to mean?"

"Captain Sisko bet me you'd thank him for the rescue *before* you started complaining."

Realizing that he as well as Dukat had been duped—Dax had maneuvered him into letting her get a dig in at the Cardassian—Sisko obliged her by saying, "I lost."

"Captain," Dukat said in a different tone, "are you aware there's a Klingon on your bridge?"

Captain, are you aware there's a scorpion crawling on your collar?

Dukat was glaring at Worf, and Worf was patently returning the glare. No love lost there.

Not feeling obliged to explain his bridge personnel to Dukat, Sisko merely said, "He's not the Klingon you should be worried about." He indicated the viewscreen and said, "Switch to aft view, maximum magnification."

The screen shimmered and changed.

And there they were—the big powerful one and the smaller mean one, coming at them like bullets.

Sisko knew that if he attempted to fire at them, it might deplete *Defiant*'s warp-core power and she might reduce her speed just enough to be caught. Better to keep up the speed, and hope DS9 was ready for a fight.

Dukat was in wide-eyed communion with the screen. "Somehow the Klingons found out my ship evacuated the council members. I'd suggest you cloak immediately."

"We lost our cloaking device rescuing you."

There was a pause.

"Can this ship go any faster?" Dukat asked.

Sisko didn't look at him. He looked only at the screen.

"Not unless you want to get out and push."

"Any luck?"

Kira Nerys hung over the Ops table, searching as she had for hours for a sign of the *Defiant*'s return. Her legs were stiff, her arms aching, and her stomach growling. Time to rest and eat?

Forget it.

I should've gone with them to the Cardassian border. That's where the action is. If I'd pushed just right, maybe Sisko would've let me come.

Imagine. Off to defend Cardassians.

The whole universe was turned upside down. Defending Cardassians whom a matter of months ago she would have relentlessly killed.

Now they would find sanctuary here, possibly even on Bajor.

Imagine that!

The Ops table was damnably silent. Sensors swept space and came up empty. Something must have gone wrong. They would've been back by now.

"Not yet." Perspiration plucking at the buff curls at his forehead, Chief O'Brien worked at his station, urging the sensors to reach a little farther, then a little farther still. "Hold on—I'm picking up something on long-range scanners. . . . It's the *Defiant!*"

"They made it!" Kira reacted. The ship was coming in uncloaked and at high speed. That meant—

"Yeah," O'Brien confirmed, "but they've got two Klingon ships on their tail." He tapped in a request for details of speed and distance, then paused. When he spoke again, it was a huff of hopeful anxiety. "The captain's hailing us!"

"On screen."

The viewscreen popped on as though excited, showing Sisko on a smoking bridge, with staggering crewmen behind him trying to maintain their posts. They'd been engaged by the enemy.

The enemy. It hardly seems real—

"Chief! Our ETA is five minutes. Are the new systems on-line?"

"Yes, sir," O'Brien answered, leaving out the part about how badly it all integrated into the Cardassian design of the station. "I wish we could've tested them first."

"No time like the present."

Without even bothering to sign off, Kira came around the Ops table. "Raise shields! Red alert!"

"Drop out of warp."

Ben Sisko gazed with hard anticipation at the viewscreen that showed the giant clawed orb of *Deep Space Nine* looming at them out of the eternal soup. It was a relief, yes, but in a nonsensical way he felt dirty for bringing the enemy down upon them. In his right mind he knew the Klingons would come here anyway, but somehow that didn't ameliorate his wish that he could've put an end to this once and for all way back on the Cardassian border, that perhaps he hadn't fought hard enough.

He shook himself out of those thoughts. "Reverse thrusters at maximum. Prepare for docking."

At his side, Dukat was an uneasy, unreassuring presence. "It looks like the Klingons chased us all this way for nothing," the Cardassian said.

"That remains to be seen. Klingons don't give up easily."

"Two ships against the station. I don't think they'd risk it."

"It may not be much of a risk," Dax put in, watching her monitors.

"What do you mean?"

"They've got friends."

Sisko pushed to his feet and came up behind Dax as the viewscreen changed, showing on its wide panorama a fleet of Klingon vessels coming out of the darkness.

Tension on the bridge doubled.

Grimly Dax reported, "The Klingon ships have raised their shields and charged their weapons."

Worf turned to Sisko. "What are your orders, Captain?"

In his mind, Sisko was already counting the ships he saw, adding up firepower and matching it against what he had in this ship around him and what the station had.

So this was how it was going to be. A couple of rogue ships attacking a Cardassian transport ship was one thing—a big thing, yes—but this was altogether different. The Klingons had trampled their treaty, and now they were shredding it.

This was not merely a diplomatic incident in a distant star system. This was an attack on a Federation outpost, and could be taken as nothing less than an act of war.

All right. So be it.

"Battle stations," he said.

CHAPTER
20

RED-ALERT KLAXONS WERE a living sound, the howl of some primitive animal brought forward into the modern age. Like the animal's noise, the klaxons signaled danger and anticipation, and the flashing red lights were like the frantic pumping of hearts in a panic.

"Status report, Major."

Sisko's voice was a low boom under the alert bells. Tense and wishing the action would get started, Kira peered into the readouts and monitors that gave them details about the Klingon fleet as it approached, then spoke up to answer his request over the sound of the red-alert noise.

"I'm detecting several dozen Klingon ships, including the *Negh'Var*," she said. "They've taken up positions just outside of weapons range."

"While you were gone," O'Brien broke in, "we

spoke to Starfleet Command. They've sent a relief force under Admiral Hastur."

"When will they get here?"

O'Brien looked at Kira, and they both realized that until now they hadn't let themselves worry about when the reinforcements would arrive. The ETA had sounded all right when Admiral Hastur reported that he was on his way. It had sounded like a relief.

Now it just sounded like a long time off.

Holding his breath, O'Brien almost choked on the answer.

"Not soon enough."

"Not soon enough is not an answer, Chief. What's their expected time of arrival?"

"I'm sorry, sir. Admiral Hastur estimated roughly an hour and a half, but said he'd try to make it sooner. The last time we were in contact with them, we ran into static. The Klingons may be scrambling signals."

Kira spoke up from where she was monitoring the approach of the Klingons. "And, sir, if the Starfleet ships run into other Klingons out there, then they'll take even longer to get here."

"Then we can't depend on them. Prepare to defend the station at all costs. Chief, what's the status of your upgrades?"

O'Brien glanced at Kira. He looked suddenly exhausted. "Everything's installed, but I have suspicions about how the Starfleet-regulation mechanics are fitting into the Cardassian housings. I've done some hard bolting-down, but full firepower makes for a lot of shaking. On top of being fired upon—"

"Understood. We'll hope for the best. Prepare to dock

the Defiant. *I want to be in Ops when this plays out. Kira?"*

Kira's arms flinched when she heard her name—a reaction that embarrassed her. "Sir?"

"Break out the sidearms, Major, stationwide. Inside or outside, we've got to be ready. We're in for the fight of our careers."

"The Klingons. First it was the Cardassians, then it was the Dominion, and now it's the Klingons. How's a Ferengi supposed to make an honest living in a place like this?"

"Come on, Quark. Move along. You should be in an emergency shelter by now."

Feeling wholly in his element as he choreographed the exit of civilians from the outer areas of the station, Odo was not surprised to find his arch-irritant still lurking about the Promenade.

Up and down the wide corridor, with all its entrances and exits, Starfleet security men and Bajoran officers directed station inhabitants toward shelters in the lower levels. The people moved with a silent resolution, not panicking, but with their faces creased by gruesome truth. They had come here under the peace established by the Federation, well away from hazard, which had been beaten back by Starfleet, and now all their structure might be collapsing, leaving those who believed themselves safe now discovering that they might have drawn the wrong straw.

Still, such was not his concern. It was not for him to tend to their emotions. At some point, all living things had to see to their own survival, whether physical or otherwise. Physically, all they had to do was cooperate with him.

The Promenade was now deserted but for Bajoran deputies standing posts with their phaser rifles.

"Quark," he began again, and approached the local underhand artist, who was wrestling a combination lock onto the closed doors of his bar.

The click of the lock was a tiny imitation of the heavy clanks and echoing booms caused by double-built airlocks closing all over the station, and the subtle irritating buzz of forcefields coming on at all the junctions.

"I'm not going to any emergency shelter," the Ferengi opposed. His face was frantic with determination. "This is my bar, and I'm going to defend it."

"Really," Odo drawled. "And how do you plan to do that?"

His animated face creased with scorn, yet somehow laced with the joy of plotting, Quark held up a box he had carried until now under his arm. Roughly the size of a place mat, the box was plain and battered, with dents on the sides and corrosion along the seams.

"With this!" he said.

Odo peered down at him with calculated ridicule. "You're going to hit them with a box?"

Quark's blue eyes bolted wide and his craggy teeth shone in his version of a joyless grin. "No, this is my disruptor pistol. The one I used to carry in the old days when I was serving on that Ferengi freighter."

"I thought you were the ship's cook."

"That's right! And every member of the crew thought he was a food critic!" He squared his thin shoulders and puffed up, even to standing on his toes. "And if the Klingons try to get through these doors, I'll be ready for them."

With the pride of a collector, and notably missing his usual false piety, he opened the case and held it before Odo, gleaming with intimidation and the solidity of being finally and utterly prepared.

Odo plucked out of the box the only thing inside— a piece of paper.

Pride dissolved from Quark's face. Shock swarmed in.

Odo squinted at the paper. "'Dear Quark . . . used parts from your disruptor to fix the replicator. Will return them soon. Your brother, Rom.'"

The box snapped shut. Quark stared at the paper in Odo's hands. "I'll kill him."

Odo looked up. "With what?"

As medieval as castle portcullises, thick airlock doors rolled shut in the crossover bridges. The boom of their weight as they closed echoed through the station's core. Armed guards rushed to posts at every junction where there wasn't a forcefield.

The Promenade, empty. The docking pylons, deserted. Living quarters, abandoned. If ever this place had been a bottle of the macabre, it was in this last hour.

The lights had been reduced in some places, to cut down on the chance of fire, but also to retard the movement of enemies who might breach the station's interior. Those who had lived here all these months could more easily function in the dim but familiar halls when things turned desperate, frantic, and bloody.

"That's close enough, Garak!"

Deep Space Nine's Cardassian-in-exile scuffed to a halt along the slight curve of the empty habitat ring, and found that it was not so empty here. As he had suspected—

He slowly approached the two Starfleet guards and the Cardassian standing between them.

"Dukat," he began, measuring his tone, "I just wanted to make sure the council members were safe."

Gul Dukat lacked his usual arrogance and today was a pillar of wariness.

"Hoping, no doubt," he challenged, "that your concern would curry political favor."

Scalded now by his own activities in the past, for which he refused to apologize, Garak cauterized, "Oh, and I take it your concern for the council members is motivated strictly by patriotism?"

"The council members are well aware of my patriotism," Dukat said, "and the sacrifices I was willing to make in order to save them. Now, why don't you go back to your tailor shop and sew something?"

"Because," Garak said forcefully, "if the Klingons do invade the station, you just may need my help."

He glanced at the Starfleet guards and their massive phaser rifles, and drew from his pocket his own small Cardassian disruptor. For an instant he enjoyed seeing terror cross Dukat's face at the sight of a weapon in Garak's hands, but Garak had no intent to use it as Dukat feared.

Yet he couldn't stand here and explain—it would

be undignified to admit that he thought they stood a good chance of dying and he wanted to die fighting, at the side of other Cardassians.

"Who would've thought the two of us would be fighting side by side?" he mentioned.

"Just be sure," Dukat said, "when you fire that thing you're firing at a Klingon."

Garak moved forward, approaching a man who, until today, had been his bane. "I'll try to keep that in mind."

Sisko stood at the top of the stairs, looking down upon his operations center. Below, the cold view of Worf handing out hand phasers and holsters to Kira, O'Brien, and Dax stirred sensations in him that he would have banished in the night had he awakened from this nightmare. *Deep Space Nine* had become that which he had always imagined it, but which it never had really been—a lone outpost, undefended, the only battlement between a raging army and the peace that had been kept for generations. He felt like Major Anderson at Fort Sumter, desperately trying not to be the man who started the American Civil War.

The inevitable war. Nothing could stop this.

Was that true? Had he sifted the sands for every possibility? Had he contacted everyone he could contact? Had he scoured his mind for every argument that might turn Gowron's mind?

Was it really too late?

The Klingons were starting a war, moving to conquer Cardassia. It seemed in many ways so natural for them to do so that he began to wonder if he had exhausted the reasons *why* they would do this. This time it was neither greed nor gamble that set the Klingons on the warpath. This time, they were afraid.

Could he use that?

As he watched his crew don their hand weapons, any such scenario eluded him. If he were Gowron, thinking the way Gowron thought . . .

"We're receiving a transmission from General Martok."

Dax's report shook Sisko out of the cloud of possibilities through which he could no longer see.

"Put him through."

He came down to the main level as the big viewscreen drew in a bigger-than-life picture of Martok—the very essence of fury, probably insulted that Sisko had not only refused to help him, but had actively and violently moved to thwart him. They weren't used to that kind of offensive action from Starfleet.

Better get used to it.

"Captain," Martok bolted as if swallowing meat. *"I demand you surrender the Cardassian council members to us immediately."*

"They're not Founders, Martok," Sisko said, controlling the sharp edges of his words. "We tested them. You were wrong."

At first he thought he'd made a grave, gut-reaction mistake by calling Martok wrong, but then saw a flicker of expectations being blasted in the Klingon general's face. He really had believed it. There wasn't any ulterior motive.

A flash of hope was dashed when, before Martok could respond, another form moved into the screen

out of the shadows of the *Negh'Var*'s bridge—
Gowron.

"It is of no consequence," the chancellor rebuffed.
*"All that matters is that the Alpha Quadrant will be
safer with the Klingon Empire in control of Cardassia.
Now . . . surrender the council members, or we will
have no choice but to take them by force."*

That said it all, yet somehow compounded what
Sisko had dreaded. Gowron meant to control his fears
by controlling Cardassia and anyone else he felt might
be at risk from Dominion infiltration.

Sisko found himself scanning the Klingon's face,
noticing flecks of metallic dust and blood. What had
happened at the border? What was Gowron doing on
Martok's ship instead of on his own? The other ship
must have been wrecked, leaving Gowron shamed
and furious—yes, it was there in his owl-like eyes.
The humiliation of having been surprised by prepared
Cardassians, of having a vessel smashed around him,
and of having to abandon its smoldering hulk, then
depend on someone else to rescue him.

We can use that, Sisko thought. *He's on edge. I can
push him over.*

He reached into his deepest, darkest, backest pocket and pulled out his last card, one he knew would get
some kind of rise out of Gowron, whether good or
bad. "And risk an all-out war with the Federation?"

Gowron's eyes blew wider and he leaned forward.
"If a war starts here, the blame will be yours."

"I doubt very much if history will see it that way."

"History is written by the victors."

Much as Sisko disliked admitting it, Gowron was
right about that. History would be unkind to the

Federation if they allowed their hard-forged peace to be shattered by a Klingon rampage with a distorted motive.

Martok spoke up again. *"Consider what you're doing, Captain. The lives of everyone on the station are at risk."*

Anger flared in Sisko's gut. What did he think they were? Huddling refugees?

"I'm aware of that," he shot back. "But maybe you're not aware of what you're risking. We've had a year to prepare this station for a Dominion attack. And we're *more* than ready."

He probably shouldn't have given them fair warning, but he felt like saying it, and any satisfaction he could get out of the next events would be sustenance.

Gowron laughed outright, as if Sisko were baiting him.

"You are like a toothless old grishnar cat, trying to frighten us with your roar!"

"I assure you this old cat isn't as toothless as you think," Sisko said, cashing in on his strong wish to tell it all. "Right now I've got five thousand photon torpedoes armed and ready to launch. If you don't believe me, feel free to scan the station."

On the screen, Martok turned to one of his bridge officers, who nodded to him. Who could tell what that meant?

Then Martok turned again, this time to face Gowron.

"It is a trick. An illusion created by thoron fields and duranium shadows."

"It's no illusion." Sisko suddenly felt very calm. If they believed Martok's report—where had he gotten false information about the station's weapons?—then they would come in too close and be cut to pieces.

Sisko could live with that.

"We shall see," Gowron said. *"ChegHchu djajVam djajKak!"*

The transmission cut off abruptly, leaving in their memories the sight of Gowron's wild icy eyes ringed with white and set in his bronze, gnarled face.

A few seconds ticked off; then Sisko automatically turned to Worf.

So did all others.

The moment turned uneasy—tainted by the shortsightedness of expecting Worf to be their token Klingon and explain to them all that they did not understand about those who attacked them now.

Worf didn't flinch under their questioning eyes. Evidently this had happened to him before.

He shifted his feet, glanced at the screen that now showed the *Negh'Var* and the other Klingon vessels sweeping in an unbroken pattern toward the station, and he seemed as separated from them as from the ship he had lost.

With careful lack of inflection, he told them, "He said, 'Today is a good day to die.'"

CHAPTER
21

"IF THAT'S THE way he wants it, that's the way we'll give it to him. Priority to weapons systems."

"Sir, that might weaken the shields."

Crawling to his feet after adjusting something in the lower trunks, O'Brien winced as he caught his finger in his phaser holster and worked it free without shooting off his whole hand.

"If we don't beat them off, the shields won't matter," Sisko said as he took a position at the Ops table to watch the approach of the Klingon ships. "Target the lead ships. Ready even-numbered photon launchers."

In his mind he saw the heavy photon cannons and multiple pump-phaser arrays on the outer sections of the station shifting into place, each section slicing out a wedge of space to defend. They were the arms of his body and the parcels of his mind as he stretched out to defend what was his.

The lead Klingon ships blew in, veered their patterns of approach to strafe the station with their disruptors, and it sounded as if a thunderstorm had broken loose outside.

No sense waiting around for the inevitable.

"Fire on my mark," Sisko said, just to get their hands on their mechanisms. "Fire."

The crew worked their various controls—and he realized how many panels it took to manipulate the number of cannons they'd installed. Worf, Kira, Dax, and three other Ops personnel were all hunching over their consoles.

From weapons arrays all over the outer perimeter, up the weapons sails and mounted on the docking rings, *Deep Space Nine* tore space apart. The sound was even more penetrating than the hits they took from the Klingon disruptors.

On the screens and smaller monitors all over Ops they could see Montana-blue bolts issue into the black sky all around the station, chasing the Klingon ships as they veered off to make another approach. The Klingons were being hit hard, their outer shields battered through by white-hot photon impact, and from the wobble of their wings, they were surprised.

That wobble gave Sisko encouragement as he swung from monitor to monitor, trying to watch all the ships at once.

"Ready odd-numbered launchers . . . fire!"

The sound of more torpedoes flung into close space echoed through Ops.

"They're still closing!" Kira called over the thrum of photon launch.

"Ready phasers," Sisko ordered evenly.

Worf turned. "Standing by."

"Fire."

Bright streaks of deadly concentrated energy threaded space like the tines of a spider's web, joining the station to its enemy's hulls and cutting through the weakened shields and into cold metal.

"Recoil is causing some structural vibrations," O'Brien called over the *thrum thrum* of effort from the new weapons. "It's the station's design, sir. I was afraid of this."

"Take note of where the weaknesses are and we'll do our shoring up later, Chief."

"If we have a later," Kira tossed in.

Sisko twisted around. "We'll have a later. Chief, what are the vibrations doing to us?"

"We could have some hull ruptures in the pylons."

"I don't care about that. What else?"

"It's shaking loose the deflector housings. If they hit us there, we could lose the shields for a couple of minutes."

"Set up a bypass in case that happens, and inform all internal defense posts to stay on their toes."

Two explosions on the monitors lit up Ops and drew attention. A second later, there was another, then one more.

"Eight Klingon ships destroyed!" Kira sang out. "Several others heavily damaged."

They watched as a new wave of attacking ships swung in, attempting to bore through the station's surprise firepower by coming in on direct lines with the station's axis.

"Contact Gowron," Sisko said. "Maybe we can put an end to this before it goes any farther."

Dax worked at her controls, then shook her head. "They're not respon—"

The station rocked hard, as if kicked from underneath.

"They've given you your answer, Captain," Worf suggested.

Sisko shook his head. Evidently Gowron had no intention of giving up yet. Of course not—other than being able to hold his own in a fight, Sisko hadn't given him a reason to quit.

There were those who said a Klingon couldn't be reasoned with. At times, plenty of times, the Klingons themselves bore up that supposition with their very actions.

He found himself looking at Worf. The big officer worked with unbroken concentration over his tactical board, his face set with determination and his wide shoulders shifting.

There had to be some reason. Something that would make sense to Gowron . . .

"Weapons stations," Sisko said grimly. "Fire at will."

Volleys of phaser fire and photon torpedoes colored the Bajoran sky and blanketed the viewscreen of the *Negh'Var* with blinding swats of light.

Gowron clutched the edge of the helm and gritted his teeth in raw frustration. In the command chair,

Martok was boiling with anger, pounding the arms of his chair and shaking his fists at his crew whenever they were forced to bear off.

At last he turned to Gowron and shouted, "They have betrayed us! They upgraded that metal knot without telling us! We were their allies!"

"They upgraded it against the Dominion," Gowron snapped back, "and were not obliged to tell us."

"But I had information that the station was unarmed!"

"From where did you get this information!"

"From the Cardassian tailor! Garak! He lives on the station! We wrenched it from him!"

"You went on board the station, assaulted one of its citizens, were given the wrong information, formed a battle strategy based upon it, and now you are mad at *them?* Martok, you stumbled! Now that your face bleeds, you blame the floor!"

Martok opened his mouth to shout a defense, but the ship was punted sideways by a direct photon hit. They both hung on as their bodies were sucked sideways by a sudden loss of gravitational stability.

"They fight like Klingons!" the general choked as he stared in bald shock at the ash-gray structure hanging in open space and the garish bolts blasting from it.

"Then they can die like Klingons," Gowron vowed. He ignored Martok and shouted at the bridge officers. "Destroy their shields! Prepare boarding parties!"

Unwilling to have his command tripped from beneath him, Martok responded, "As you recommend," then did his own shouting at the comm unit. "All ships! Concentrate fire on their shield generators!"

* * *

"They've disabled two of our shield generators!" Dax's shout knelled disaster.

Chief O'Brien dodged to enable his bypasses, but the Klingons were ready.

Shimmering pillars of energy appeared around Ops—a half-dozen of them. Even before the Klingon boarding party was fully materialized, Sisko and Worf were on the move.

Sisko shouted a warning to Kira, and Worf opened fire, blowing one of the Klingons to the deck just as the invader became solid. Good thing, too, because Dax was right behind that Klingon. Sisko couldn't tell if Worf knew what he was doing or was just lucky with his timing, but he put all his bets on the former and moved to defend his command center.

Beside him as he accepted the brutal tackle of another Klingon, Kira opened fire on one of them across the deck while Dax engaged another one with whatever she could of her martial-arts knowledge, though it was crimped by the lack of space here.

As Sisko's throat throbbed in the Klingon's elbow, he had to endure watching another Klingon knock Kira's phaser from her hands then set into her with a dagger.

While the blade was embedded in her side, Kira took advantage and rammed the Klingon in the eye with her elbow. As the pain drove him back, Kira swung around and let her boot heel do the rest of her talking. Then she slid out of sight behind the Ops table.

How many of them were there?

* * *

A shimmer of transporter light buzzed in the Promenade, where no one ever directly transported, and suddenly Odo found himself dodging the strike of a Klingon *bat'leth*. The vicious curved weapon made a *shussh* as it washed past him, its sharp tines flickering under the corridor lighting.

Battling down his own surprise, Odo ducked under the Klingon's arm and counterattacked, using what his other friends regarded as superior strength. Perhaps because he was not muscle and bone that could be too easily crushed or snapped, he had some advantage. But this Klingon and the one right behind him were upon him so fast that he had no chance to think of any physical advantages he might have.

As they both cornered him and attacked him, he almost shapeshifted to his natural form, the gelatinous liquid that made him so out of place here, but he thought better of it. If he shifted here and now, and these Klingons managed to get away, the rumor would fly through the Klingon ranks that there were shapeshifters on *Deep Space Nine,* and any negotiations Captain Sisko was planning would be blasted away.

So he fought with all his physical ability and his mental will, taking blow upon blow across his head and shoulders. Each blow left him numb in that place and he tried to dodge fast enough to make the Klingons' own plunges work against them.

For a few moments, it worked. Then the Klingons realized what he was doing and began to work as a team rather than two random attackers.

One of them pulled him back, off his own center of balance, and the other raised his weapon—

A bolt of phaser fire crackled down the Promenade—at first Odo thought he was hit.

Then the Klingons tensed, and fell backward without checking their falls.

Stunned!

Only half believing that he was free of these two, Odo spun around and shuddered with the effort he had expended.

From down the Promenade, Julian Bashir gazed at him, holding his phaser.

"Thank you, Doctor," Odo said.

Bashir nodded. "Anytime."

"Have you seen any others?" Odo fell in step with him and led the way around the great wide curve.

"Not personally," the doctor said, "but I heard sounds of struggling and energy discharge near turboshaft D. I was coming to get you."

"We'll secure the Promenade before we report to Captain Sisko."

"That might not be so easy, if the shields are down and they're able to beam in anywhere."

Odo made a disapproving sound in his throat. "I didn't let the Cardassians come back here once they were thrown out, and I have no intention of letting the Klingons have this station. If I have to turn into a bulkhead and fall on them one by one, Doctor, believe me, I'll do it."

Of all the doorways on *Deep Space Nine,* only one led to the quarters where the Cardassian council members were under guard. Because that doorway was so heavily guarded, it was easy to find, and the Klingons found it.

There, Garak stood side by side with Dukat, bleeding, bruised, breathless, as they wrestled for their lives with four Klingon warriors.

The two Federation guards were on the ground, dead, along with the three other Klingons they had taken with them, and the carpet was mushy with blood as it drained and mixed.

Beside him, Dukat somehow got a grip on a *bat'leth* and was hacking at two Klingons so viciously that blood ran like grape juice down both invaders' body armor.

Finally one of the Klingons had enough and charged Garak, driving him up against the locked door panel. While Dukat and his opponent waltzed by, joined by the blows of the *bat'leth,* Garak endured the pressure of the Klingon's elbow against his skull.

Abruptly then, the Klingon was hurled backward, arms and legs cast out before him, spine arched, as he struck the opposite bulkhead. A gaping gouge in his stomach burned with enduring energy.

Garak immediately turned, clutching the disruptor he had taken from his opponent, and swung around to the other Klingons, picked one, and fired.

"All this hand-to-hand combat is really quite distasteful," he panted, secretly enjoying Dukat's struggle with the *bat'leth* as one of the Klingons tried to take it away.

"I suppose," Dukat gulped, "you prefer the simplicity of an interrogation chamber."

A second Klingon was on Dukat now, leaving one for Garak.

But he was ready, and he fired directly into the

Klingon's face just before he himself might have been cut in half by another advancing *bat'leth*.

"You have to admit, it's much more civilized," Garak heaved out. His chest felt as if someone were standing on it.

"All right," Dukat hurled back as he threw off one of the Klingons and swung to deal with the other. "I can arrange one for you!"

Enraged by what he saw, Sisko gripped the arm of his enemy around his throat and managed to use the big alien's weight against him. Pivoting, he threw the Klingon to the deck. As he straightened, he saw another Klingon nail O'Brien with a brutal kick. As the chief went down, the Klingon's victory was cut off by one of those Klingon weapons—in the hands of Worf.

Worf cut into the Klingon with a combination of blows that left the invader pulp-faced and on the deck.

Worf's face was wild with fury as he swung around and looked for another opponent. It was terrible and wonderful to see.

Blinking at a dribble of sweat running into his eye—or was it blood?—Sisko found an angle that put him and Worf back to back, though there was more than twelve feet between them.

Around them, only Starfleet people were conscious—not healthy, but awake. For a moment, Sisko didn't believe it.

Worf immediately dropped back into his seat at the weapons-control panel, and Dax took Kira's place.

Sisko snapped his fingers at two of the security

guards who were still on their feet and gestured for them to secure the unconscious Klingons. Maybe they were dead Klingons. Didn't matter. He wanted them out of the way.

He stepped over one of them to get to O'Brien and pull the dazed engineer to his feet. "Mr. O'Brien, get those shields back on-line."

The chief shook off the punch he'd taken and staggered to his station with a muttered affirmative.

Sisko didn't wait to see if he made it, but stepped to Kira, who now lay on the deck with a knife wound in her side.

"Major?" he began as he knelt there. His stomach twisted as he saw the blood seeping between her fingers.

"I'll be okay," she said quickly. "It's not as bad as it looks."

Maybe, maybe not. Sisko didn't have time to do anything more than take her at her word.

He struck his comm badge. "Sisko to Odo!"

"Odo here."

"Status report."

"We have Klingon troops on the Promenade, the habitat ring, and lower pylon three. We seem to have them contained for the moment, but I can't guarantee they'll stay that way."

"Keep me informed."

There wasn't anything else to say. The guards down there would just have to do their best on their own.

Worf twisted toward him without taking his hands off his controls. "There's another wave of Klingon ships coming in."

"I've got the shields back up," O'Brien gasped, "but I don't know how long they'll stay up."

Dax fought to steady her breath as she gazed into her own monitors, and a single crease of worry damaged her perfect brow.

She turned to Sisko, her eyes tight.

"I'm reading a cluster of warp signatures approaching," she said with unproclaimed foreboding, "bearing one-eight-seven mark zero-two-five."

And she continued to look at him.

His body heavy and his mind frayed, Sisko came up behind her. Together they looked at the empty main viewer, which in seconds would no longer be empty.

In the center of the screen, faint white dots of approaching ships began to appear.

CHAPTER
22

BEN SISKO WATCHED the tiny dots on the main screen, and his chest began to feel empty. With additional ships coming in, the Klingons would have the advantage. At some point in every contest, nobility no longer served, and stamina began to slacken.

This was that moment. It had come before in his career, and he recognized the snag in his throat and the hollow under his ribs. The last time he had possessed no recourse, nothing to deprive the enemy of victory if he could not have it himself. This time he did.

He had fusion reactors.

When the Klingon ships moved in as close as he believed they would, flexing their pecs and showing their triceps, he would lure as many near as he could, and then—

Blow up the station. He made himself say it in his mind. *Blow up the station, blow up the station.*

He calculated how many people were left on the station now, how many had been evacuated, where his son was and what Jake would think when, from the planet's surface, he saw the unnatural fireball bloom in the Bajoran sky. Later there would be the grieving, and all Sisko could hope was that Jake was old enough to overcome resentment and realize that his dad had sacrificed himself and the station, and in fact most of their best friends, to take out a large portion of the Klingon fleet, but also to send that critical message to the Klingons—Starfleet's not kidding.

Think, Gowron. How can I make you think? What can I do to make you perceive the whole fabric of what's coming? How can I break through your fears? There's got to be something in Klingon legend that involves backing off!

Martok might be a factor. He was just plain insulted that the Cardassian council had been snatched out from under him. For him, the future was the half hour and the goal was to ravage and take DS9 and humiliate Sisko.

Surely, though, there was more to Gowron. It was he who would bear the brunt of the next hour's actions, and the thunder that came after. Perhaps there was still a way to pit them against each other.

Sisko looked across Ops at Worf. He saw the conflict there and the fact that reason was winning out. It could happen.

Having Worf at his side somehow boosted his spirits, even now. Reason . . . not muscle. That was it. The chance of fighting the Klingons down was over—they'd have to be talked down, and cut off the battle of their own volition.

Sisko parted his lips to ask Dax for a tie-in to Gowron, but the chance was stolen when Dax suddenly straightened and looked up at the dots on the main screen.

"They're Starfleet, Benjamin!" she said brightly. "Six starships, led by the *Venture!* They'll be here in fifteen minutes!"

A second chance! Sisko felt his eyes go wide, then fought to control his reaction. He still had a certain image to maintain, for the sake of those who would no doubt fight at his side again someday.

"Try to contact the *Negh'Var* again," he said with much more vigor than he would've said it a moment ago. "Maybe now Gowron will be in the mood to talk."

Because now I've got something to hold at his throat.

"I've got him." Dax was apparently ready before he'd said anything. Good crew.

The screen dropped the incoming ships and picked up a stony-faced Gowron and Martok.

"Captain," Gowron attempted, "your shields have been weakened, your station boarded, and more Klingon ships are on the way. Surrender while you can."

Strange the way he said it—as though in their acquaintance he might have picked up the idea that Sisko wouldn't surrender to him.

Gowron looked dashed, but not surprised, when Sisko puffed up before him.

"I don't think so. My shields are holding, your

boarding parties have been contained, and *my* reinforcements are closer than yours. Gowron . . . you're facing a war on two fronts. Is that what you really want?"

Without looking away from the screen, he raised his hand to Worf and made a silent gesture.

Worf turned fully to the screen and added, "The Klingon Empire isn't strong enough to fight the Federation *and* the Cardassians. End this now . . . before you lead the Empire to its worst defeat in history."

That was it—the key to Gowron. Sisko realized that he and Worf had discovered it at the same instant. The Empire—the Founders—the very core of Klingon fear and the reason they were launching this conflict.

As if sensing what was happening, Martok leaned forward on the screen and bellowed, *"We will not surrender!"*

This idiot would blow everything yet, if Sisko let him get the upper hand. Upper wind.

"I'm sure the Founders will be very happy to hear that," Sisko said evenly, but with a certain force. "That is exactly what the Founders want. Klingon against Cardassian, Federation against Klingon . . . The more we fight, the weaker we'll get, and the less chance we'll have against the Dominion."

With his manner he indicated that he would indeed go on fighting, until *Deep Space Nine* was left a scattered cloud of metallic dust, and then no one, not even the Klingons, would have any way of guarding the wormhole. The Dominion could come through unstayed. Then what?

"Consider what you do here, Gowron," Worf went

on, pointedly ignoring Martok as if his opinion were no voice at all. "Kahless himself said, 'Destroying an Empire to win a war is no victory.'"

Gowron's cheeks flushed magenta to have his own legends tossed back in his face. Clearly things weren't working out as he had planned, or as he had been led to believe they could.

"And ending a battle to save an Empire is no defeat," he finished.

Sisko couldn't tell if that was the rest of the quotation, or something new Gowron was just realizing, but he liked the sound of it.

Martok put the last nail in the coffin of his own hopes by shouting to Gowron, *"But we can still win!"*

He sounded childish, foolish, desperate, and all but stomped his foot in a tantrum.

"Not before those starships get here," Sisko reminded them coolly. "Now . . . what do I tell them? To stand down? Or come in firing?"

He liked the sound of that, and he enjoyed saying it.

He also enjoyed watching reality crawl across Gowron's face. No one, not even an enraged and frightened Klingon, took lightly the prospect of taking on a handful of Starfleet's heavy cruisers.

"No," Gowron said with nearly physical effort. *"It is we who will stand down."*

On the screen, Martok shouted something in Klingon, sounding as if he were sneezing real hard.

Gowron snapped to his side. *"Enough! Cease fire! Order your ships in Cardassian territory to halt their advance! I do not intend to hand victory to the Dominion!"* Still enflamed, he swung back to Sisko. *"But let your people know—the Klingon Empire will remem-*

ber what has happened here. You have sided against us in battle." For the last, he pointed across open space at Worf. *"And this we cannot forgive . . . or forget."*

The transmission ended, like a light snapping off.

A few seconds of tension plied the station's operational center as all the crew held their breath, to see if the Klingons were enacting some deception and would turn on them anyway while they had paused to talk.

But a few moments later Dax said, "The Klingons are powering down their weapons."

Weak with relief, O'Brien uttered, "It's over. . . ."

Over. And they were still alive.

Then Worf turned to them, and there was scant comfort in his expression.

"For now," he said.

CHAPTER
23

Captain's Log, Stardate 49011.4. Damage-control teams have completed repairs to the station, and life is beginning to return to normal. Most of the civilian citizens have been brought back from the planet's surface, the Promenade and habitat ring have received security clearance and are open again, the Cardassian council has been remanded to Starfleet Command for protection until Cardassia Prime's section of space can be further stabilized, and Quark has reopened his bar. As far as Deep Space Nine is concerned, the latter is as good an indication of normality as any, and better than some. I am left with only one final piece of unfinished business.

"Mr. Worf, I brought you your discharge papers."

Worf's quarters had an aura of the temporary as Sisko strolled in. These were simple guest quarters, but reserved for Starfleet personnel or Bajoran officials, and therefore were Spartan and unadorned. There was neither a sense of welcome or farewell here.

In civilian clothing and therefore somewhat incongruous with his nature, Worf stood at the bed, packing his bags. Inadvertently Sisko had caught him just putting away his Starfleet uniform, and if instincts were worth anything, Sisko thought the Klingon officer had been staring a few seconds too long at the uniform.

Could be imagination. Or hope.

Sisko held out the padd with the images of Worf's discharge orders. "I thought you might want to look at them before I send them off to Starfleet."

Sometimes that worked.

"I understand you're headed for the Nyberrite Alliance," he added slowly.

Worf nodded. "I leave this afternoon."

Nothing in his manner suggested that he was looking forward to leaving, or that he was satisfied with his decision. Was this how it must be for those with each foot in a different culture?

Sisko sighed. "For me, it was a job on Earth, directing the construction of orbital habitats."

Worf looked up, almost hopeful. "Why did you change your mind?"

Pacing away to give his words room to mill, Sisko ran his hand along the edge of the dresser. "I finally realized it wasn't Starfleet I wanted to get away from. I was trying to escape from my wife's death. I thought I could just wrap the uniform around the pain . . . and toss them both away."

He chose his words with great care, yet felt as if he

had said them before, over and over again in his inner mind.

"But it doesn't work like that. Running may help for a little while, but sooner or later the pain catches up to you. The only way to get rid of it is to stand your ground and face it."

Not exactly a lesson in deep philosophy, he realized as he heard his own words. In fact, these were the first thoughts to come to his mind. None of this, he knew, was anything Worf didn't realize or hadn't thought of before, but sometimes there was help in just hearing somebody else voice the plague of thoughts that were hurtful in their commonality. It helped to have someone say that he'd been there before and survived.

Survive . . . so many colors to that word. They had survived what might have been the end of peace in the quadrant, yet now they had to endure the lasting tension that had sprung up. Survive death, or survive someone else's death . . . or a ship's death, or a career's . . . to survive with one's spirit intact was itself a victory.

"But wearing the uniform," Worf slowly broke into Sisko's thoughts, "only reminds you of what you have lost."

"Sometimes," Sisko admitted. "But it also reminds me of what I've gained and who I am. I'm a Starfleet officer. I could throw away my uniform, resign my commission, and run all the way to the Nyberrite Alliance, and it wouldn't make any difference. That's what I am, and that's what I'll always be."

And my wife will always be dead and the Enterprise *will always be gone. Get over it.*

Worf narrowed his eyes, clinging to what he was being forced to hear, as if he had avoided what he damned well knew.

"And you think that is true of me as well."

Realizing he might have overstepped, Sisko said, "What's important, Mr. Worf, is what you think."

Worf gazed down at the uniform he hadn't quite been able to stuff away. "I think Starfleet has been my home for many years. And perhaps it still is."

He wasn't surprised. None of this was a revelation. He seemed merely to be accepting what he already knew, now that he heard someone else admit to knowing it. A broken heart was a strange but simple thing.

"There are starships out there," Sisko ventured, "that need good officers. In fact, the captain of the *Venture* is a friend of mine. If you'd like, I could talk to him . . . see if he has an opening for a lieutenant commander."

Pulling the uniform out of the duffel bag and holding it in both hands in front of him, Worf turned to face Sisko.

"Perhaps that will not be necessary," he said.

Boreth Monastery. Well-named, for Worf was barely inside the sixteen-foot courtyard doors before he was already bored and glad he had no intention of staying.

It was good that this place was out in the middle of nothing instead of on the homeworld, for he would not go there now.

He was only barely welcome here, for word was spreading that he had stayed with Starfleet when the

Klingon cause had summoned him, then aided Starfleet in its "betrayal" of Klingon intents, though he had never made any secret of where his allegiance would go as long as he wore the uniform.

And he still wore it today. He felt proud, glad to be wearing it as he strode in here today, for by doing so he was openly defying all the threats and posturing against him.

The clerics stared as he strode through in his forbidden livery, still wearing over his Starfleet uniform the bandoleer of his Klingon heritage.

Without a glance he walked past all the places where he had sought comfort before and not found it.

He went straight to the inner abbey, and there he found the one face he sought across a quarter of the quadrant and across two guarded borders. Some things were worth a border run.

"Lourn."

"Brother Worf! I heard rumors you were coming, but I didn't believe it. I'm surprised you've come so deep into your home space, considering what is being said about you."

"What is being said about me is true. When my moment of choice came, I chose against the Empire. And this is not my home space, and I am not your brother. I have come here to comfort myself by telling you what I have learned, so you will no longer plague my thoughts as I do my job.

"I am here to tell you that you are wrong. You should stop teaching our warriors to never question what they do. Everything you have been teaching here is what has nearly destroyed us. Don't think—just do."

"Worf . . . you surely must be confused."

"Not any longer. I have a post again, and I have a new commanding officer. No one is lost who has that. And I saw something happen which made me come here today. I watched as Captain Sisko discovered that the Klingon decision to attack the Cardassians was based not upon boldness, but on fear."

"Fear?" Lourn's small eyes flared and his brow ridge puckered. "In the Klingon fleet? I'm disappointed that you carry a tale like that. We were willing to take on the changelings! What's more brave than that? Sisko is mistaken."

"He is not mistaken. I saw the truth for myself, and my eyes were opened. There were never any changelings. Gowron and the High Council acted on empty fear and rumors when the Cardassian revolution came. They moved against those who were not enemies. They reacted the way Klingons react when they feel threatened. Lourn, it is the way you and the others here are teaching our warriors to behave. Attack something. Anything. And that is what occurred. When they felt threatened, the Klingons acted like children. They attacked anything in sight, including the Federation. That is exactly what the Dominion would want, and the Empire nearly handed it to them."

Lourn blinked as if stricken. He squinted at Worf, trying to peer under the mask to see what mad alien had taken Worf's identity to come here and say these things.

Scrapes on the walls and within the bare archways gave away the presence of others, students and clerics who were drawn by the excitement of Worf's daring presence and who now peered in at the two and listened.

Lourn seemed affected by the fact that they had an audience, and that whatever they said here would not be private, but also by the fact that Worf didn't seem to care.

"Our solidarity has given us survival, Worf," he insisted, speaking fiercely, but there was a quaver in his voice. "Our past is heavy with tales of—"

"Yes, I know what our past says." Nodding in token appreciation for history, Worf said, "While this may have helped us survive on some inhospitable planet long ago, we cling to it in the wrong times. We still act like children. And this time, by alienating the Federation, we may have ruined our best chance for surviving what the future brings. In our solidarity we may have caused such a disruption that others will have to destroy us. Because we were so afraid, we had to attack someone. Now we can no longer stand together against the Dominion. To oppose that, I am going to still be a Klingon, but I am a better Klingon, for I am working toward our true survival. You were wrong to teach me that I should be ashamed of going beyond my nature. That is what intelligence is for. I am no less Klingon because I stay in Starfleet. There is nothing you can teach me. In fact, you could learn much from me."

Lourn stared and stared, for he had very likely never heard phrases like these in his entire life.

As he shredded the cleric's pulpit, Worf understood that he might be called cruel, but there was too much at stake. A generation of young Klingons would come here, and they deserved to hear the facts of the open galaxy.

"Go out into the stars, Lourn," he said. "Remove your robes and leave these courtyards, and go out. Become more than you are. We must be more than our songs and legends if we are to flourish. A race that cannot get along with others will be its own death."

His face chalky and his hand trembling, Lourn breathed in shallow gusts through his open mouth. He stared at Worf, then at the flagstones beneath them, then at Worf again.

"But . . . we are Klingons!" Lourn insisted, flaring his hands between them, to engulf the peering eyes and straining ears around them.

With patent diminishment, Worf shook his head. "Is that all you can think of to say?"

His mouth dry as dust, Lourn stood shuddering in his robes that now hung on him as rags hang on a hook. His eyes were hollow, his icons shattered, and it would be his thoughts from now on that would be plagued.

At last Worf felt complete. He took a step backward that signaled his time to leave this place and go back to his post, to the people with whom he had things in common.

"I will always be Klingon," he finished calmly, "but now, I am *more* than Klingon."

EPILOGUE

"LIEUTENANT COMMANDER WORF reporting for duty, sir."

Such victory—over his own fears, he realized. The words flowed as easily as ever. There was no taint upon them, no bitter taste, no twinge of mistake.

The uniform he wore was no longer the gold of Security, but the red of Command.

After all, a man had to make *some* changes now and then.

In the Ops center, Captain Sisko gazed up at him. "You all know our new Strategic Operations Officer," he said with flair.

Around Worf, new eyes beamed at him also, but he realized that in fact they were no longer the eyes of people he didn't know. They were O'Brien and Major Kira, Jadzia Dax and Dr. Bashir. And even Odo offered a controlled nod that reassured Worf he was welcome.

His mind blurred with self-consciousness as they uttered phrases to him that made him feel good—

"Welcome aboard . . ."

"Congratulations . . ."

"Glad to have you here . . ."

Almost as if he hadn't been here—or was somehow reborn here.

As Worf stepped down, Sisko let the welcomes echo, then said, "Assume your post, Mr. Worf."

"Yes, sir," Worf said.

His post was next to O'Brien's engineering station, and that was an added sustenance for him. He had already plunged into the soup, and now he would have the chance to ease in with a little less attention focused on him. He would have the chance to get to know this station, its purpose, its mission, and the responsibilities that fate, government, and science had dropped at its distant door.

After all, this was still the deepest of space.

Captain Sisko scanned his crew as if to gain a sense of balance.

"Now that everyone's here, I wanted to let you all know that I just spoke to Dukat and several members of the Detepa Council. They've returned to Cardassia Prime without incident and asked me to convey to you their personal thanks."

Kira shook her head. "Who would've thought I'd help save the Cardassian government?"

"Don't worry," Odo told her. "I'm sure Dukat will take all the credit."

"Poor Garak," Bashir put in. "Dukat's a hero, and he's still stuck in his tailor shop, hemming pants."

Dax interrupted their banter. "Captain, I'm receiving a Priority One message from Starfleet Intelligence." She turned and looked at him. "The Klingons are refusing to give up several of the Cardassian colonies they seized during the invasion. They're fortifying their positions . . . and deploying orbital defense systems."

No one looked at Worf, but he felt their hearts turn to him. He had made his effort to spread the word to the Klingons, and could only hope that in time it *would* spread. Until then, he had new people to get to know, a new situation with which to become familiar, and a hundred new dimensions of function and espionage that made up this place called *Deep Space Nine*.

He would have to pay close attention.

As if she had forgotten he was here, Kira looked at the main screen and sighed. "Looks like the Klingons are here to stay."

In the disquieting moment of tension, Ben Sisko gave Worf a sidelong glance and a tenor of determination.

"Maybe they are," he said. "But so are we."